Just Another Pretty Face

CANDACE SCHULER

MILLS & BOON LIMITED
ETON HOUSE, 18-24 PARADISE ROAD
RICHMOND, SURREY TW9 1SR

First published in Great Britain in 1994
by Mills & Boon Limited, Eton House, 18-24 Paradise Road,
Richmond, Surrey TW9 1SR

© Candace Schuler 1993

ISBN 0 263 78849 0

21 - 9409

Printed in Great Britain by
BPC Paperbacks Ltd

"I know several effective ways of disabling a man."

"Do you?" Pierce asked, bending his head to take her mouth with his.

Shock held Nikki stock-still for a long, delicious moment. Then the heat of his mouth got through to her, his casual expertise and unmistakable, instinctive carnality touching a deeply buried nerve, and she felt herself begin to respond. Panicked, she slid her booted foot behind his bare ankle and pushed against his chest with both hands.

He went down like a running back who'd been sandwiched between two opposing players coming in opposite directions.

"I told you not to—" Nikki began hotly, and then she shrieked as he scissored his feet around her legs and brought her tumbling down to join him on the floor. She felt his arms lock around her, pinning hers to her sides as he rolled on top of her. Obviously, the martial arts moves he displayed on-screen weren't all for show. She cursed and struggled.

"Is that the best you can do?" he inquired politely, his eyes twinkling with amusement— and arousal.

Nikki glared at him. "If I wasn't afraid of doing some permanent damage to that twelve-million-dollar hide of yours," she hissed, "I'd show you what I can do."

Dear Reader,

LIGHTS, CAMERA, ACTION!

Join with Temptation as the drama continues to unfold
in popular author Candace Schuler's **Hollywood
Dynasty**. Meet the Kingston family—box-office
legends in front of and behind the cameras. Share in the
revelation of intimate secrets and the struggle for
success in this behind-the-scenes blockbusting mini-
series.

Meet film star and sex symbol Pierce Kingston this
month as he vetoes his overprotective sister's idea that
he needs a bodyguard, despite the threatening letters he's
been receiving. What need could he have for his new
"shadow"—a tall, incredibly gorgeous brunette!

Look out for THE RIGHT DIRECTION—a coming
attraction in October 1994.

The Editor
Mills & Boon Temptation
Eton House
18-24 Paradise Road
Richmond
Surrey
TW9 1SR

1

"AW, COME ON, Claire. A bodyguard?" Pierce Kingston, his six feet, three inches of muscled masculine pulchritude sprawled across an overstuffed red chintz sofa in the garden room of his Beverly Hills mansion, looked up at his sister with an expression of mild distaste on his classically handsome face. "Isn't that a little extreme? It's only a few weird fan letters. I've had weird fan letters before."

"Not this weird," Claire said, gesturing toward the half-a-dozen letters spread out on the free-form cypress-and-glass coffee table. They looked innocuous enough. The lined notepaper was pale blue. The ink was aqua. The flowing feminine script was full of fancy curlicues and swirls. Claire sighed heavily. "I know they look as if they were written by some love-struck little teenager—"

"I don't know," said Pierce, wrinkling his nose at the musky exotic scent that wafted up from the pastel notepaper. "That perfume is kind of heavy for anyone much under thirty-five to wear."

"—but they were written by someone with an unbalanced mind," Claire continued, ignoring his interruption. "Someone who's completely lost her grasp on reality."

"That doesn't mean it still couldn't be a teenager." Gage, the third and eldest Kingston sibling, spoke up from his seat on the arm of one of the other chintz sofas. "Lots of teenagers have unbalanced minds."

Claire gave him a cool, narrow-eyed look, the one that had caused the tabloids to christen her the Ice Queen of Hollywood when she was barely twenty-one years old.

"Well, they do," he insisted. "Have you listened to what passes for love songs these days among the high-school crowd? Some of it's sick stuff." He shook his head mournfully. "Very sick."

Claire turned her gaze to the lovely strawberry blonde sitting with Gage's arm draped around her shoulders. "Make him behave," she said to her brother's wife.

Tara Channing-Kingston put a slender hand on her husband's knee. "Behave," she ordered sternly, turning her head to smile up at him as she said it.

Gage smiled back at her. "For you—" he lifted his hand from her shoulder to brush his fingers through her hair "—anything," he said, and bent to kiss her.

"Gawd, isn't that just too sweet for words?" Pierce drawled, pretending to be offended by his brother and sister-in-law's unselfconscious display of affection. "Haven't you two been married long enough to stop playing kissy-face in public?" He glanced over at his sister. "It's no wonder she's pregnant again," he said, and shook his head. "And little Beau barely a year old."

"You're just jealous," Gage said complacently, settling his arm back around his wife's shoulders.

"Jealous?" Pierce scoffed. "Ha! The day I'm jealous of a poor ol' married geezer like you is—"

"*Do you mind?*" Claire said in a carefully measured voice. "I'm trying to discuss something serious here."

Both brothers sobered instantly. They knew that tone. It was her annoyed producer's voice, the one their younger sister used to quell arguments from recalcitrant directors and fractious actors. She'd inherited it directly from their formidable mother. "Sorry," they mumbled in unison.

"Can I go on now?"

"Yes, of course." Pierce made a graceful, placating gesture with one hand. "Please continue."

"Thank you. Now, as I was saying, whoever wrote those letters knows entirely too much about your movements for my peace of mind. Her last letter makes it clear that she knew all about the AIDS benefit Elizabeth Taylor hosted last week."

"It was very well publicized," Pierce pointed out. "That was the whole idea."

"She knew about the dinner you hosted at Spago beforehand, too."

"Spago is a public place. Anyone could have seen me there. *With* Alanna Fairchild," he added, referring to the model he was currently dating in an effort to forestall his sister's next argument.

"She also knew you brought Alanna back here after the benefit for a private party of your own," Claire reminded him. "And that wasn't in any paper that I know of."

"It was an easy enough assumption to make, though. Alanna and I have been seeing each other off and on for—what?—three months now?"

"Not quite one month," Claire said. "But that's beside the point."

"Just one month?" It seemed longer to him, somehow. "Are you sure?"

"Positive," Claire said dryly. "Can we get on with this?"

"I don't see that there's anything to get on with."

Claire sighed in exasperation. "Pierce."

"Well, I don't," he insisted. "Those letters are from some poor deluded woman who thinks she's in love with the man she sees on the movie screen. And she thinks I'm that man. It's sad, I'll admit, and a little creepy, but you've got to admit that it isn't unusual. I get weird stuff in the mail all the time. Besides," he added, "this woman's been writing to me for at least a year and you never said anything about a bodyguard before."

"Damn it, Pierce, that 'poor deluded woman' threatened to kill you in her last letter," Claire said, picking up a sheet of pale blue paper to shake at him. "And a bodyguard just might keep her from getting close enough to do it."

There was a moment of silence as they pondered her words.

"Aren't you overreacting just a little?" Pierce suggested, trying to soothe his sister. "She didn't actually say anything about killing me."

"*I know the other women don't really mean anything to you,*" Claire said in answer, reading aloud from the letter she held. "*I know that, deep in your heart of hearts, I am your one and only true love but I just can't bear the pain of another empty betrayal. I'll do anything I have to do to stop it from happening again. Anything. Even if it means losing you forever.*" She looked up at her brother. "That certainly sounds like a threat to me."

"She sounds like a scorned lover," Tara said to no one in particular. "As if she knows Pierce—or *has* known him—intimately."

"Well, hell," Gage said, "if you're going to use Pierce's love life as a starting place . . ." He snorted in amused disgust. "Half the women in Hollywood have known him intimately."

"Not half," Pierce demurred modestly, doing his part to make light of the situation and erase the twin expressions of concern from his sister and sister-in-law's faces. "All right, maybe half," he conceded with a lopsided grin. "But most of them are still friends and none of them *ever* had any illusions about being my 'one and only true love,'" he added, looking completely, comically horrified at the prospect.

The two women ignored their menfolk's efforts to shelter them. "Have you talked to the police about this?" Tara asked her sister-in-law.

Claire shook her head. "I've made a few discreet inquiries, of course," she said, "but there's nothing the police can do at this point. Even if we knew who she is—which, of course, we don't—they couldn't do anything. Not unless she did something first. *And* there were witnesses or they caught her at it."

"Do you think one bodyguard will be enough?"

"The one I've hired is highly qualified, but that doesn't mean I've ruled out the need for a full security staff if it looks like it's necessary."

His sister's words brought Pierce out of his casual slouch. "Wait just a minute here," he said, sitting up and planting his bare feet on the floor. "I thought you called this family powwow to decide whether there was any need for a bodyguard, not to announce that you'd already hired one."

"Those—" she gestured at the letters again "—have already established the need."

"So you just went ahead and hired a bodyguard without even talking to me about it first?"

"I'm talking to you about it now."

"After the fact."

"You wouldn't have agreed with me before the fact, would you?"

"Which doesn't justify your going behind my back and—"

Claire held up a slender hand to stop him. "Just listen to me for a minute, all right? If you don't agree with me after I've had my say, then I'll agree to fire the bodyguard and let you handle this however you want," she said mendaciously. "Okay?"

Pierce hesitated, suspicious of such an easy capitulation on his sister's part. She usually put up more of a fight before she gave in. *If* she gave in. Bulldog stubbornness was another thing she'd inherited from their mother. "Okay," he said finally, his blue eyes wary. "Talk."

"If someone had written fan letters like these to Tara, what would you do?"

Pierce's outraged expression answered for him.

"Exactly," Claire said, before he could express his reaction in words. "You'd take immediate steps to protect her."

"Tara's a woman."

Claire lifted a perfectly arched eyebrow. "So?"

"So, she'd be more vulnerable in a situation like this."

"And you're invulnerable, is that it? The big strong macho man impervious to the very same things that would spell mortal danger to a mere woman?"

"Now, don't try to make this some kind of women's liberation issue, Claire. It doesn't have anything to do with equal rights."

His sister snorted inelegantly. "Then you must be beginning to believe your publicity."

"It has nothing to do with my publicity, either, damn it. And you know it. It has to do with the basic, inescapable physical differences between men and women."

Her eyebrow rose higher.

Pierce shot a glance at his brother. "Help me out here, Gage. You know what I mean."

"Uh-uh. I'm not getting into this argument," Gage said, shaking his head. He glanced down at his wife. "I have no desire to sleep in my own guest room."

"Coward," Pierce said scornfully, and turned back to his sister with the put-upon air of a man trying to be reasonable under extremely trying circumstances. "A woman is more vulnerable in a situation like this because the person writing the letters would be a man," he said, as if he were explaining the mysteries of the universe to a backward child. "And the inescapable fact is, men are bigger than women. And stronger. It's not the same when it's the other way around. There's less of a threat. Hell," he said, speaking with the easy assurance of a man bigger, stronger and more physically fit than most other men, "in most cases, I'd say the threat is practically nonexistent."

"Unless the woman has a gun."

"Those letters didn't say anything about a gun," Pierce snapped, exasperated with her.

"I'm sure Rebecca Schaeffer's murderer didn't say anything about a gun in his fan letters, either," Claire shot back, equally exasperated with him. "But that doesn't make her any less dead."

Brother and sister glared at each other for a full ten seconds.

"Aw, jeez, Claire," Pierce said finally, deciding to take another tack. "Have you thought of what the tabloids will say if some no-neck sumo wrestler in a bad suit starts following me around with a .357 Magnum strapped to his hip?"

She fixed her brother with a gimlet stare. "Since when have you started caring about what the tabloids say?"

"Since never," Pierce said airily. "But as one of the head honchos at Kingston Productions, you certainly should—because what they'll say is that I've wimped out and hired a baby-sitter." A crafty light entered what the press liked to call his 'laserlike baby blues.' "*The Devil's Game* will be premiering next month," he said, referring to his latest movie. "Think what effect that kind of negative publicity could have on the box office."

"I have thought about it," Claire said.

"Aha," he crowed, sensing victory. "I knew I could make you see reason."

"That's why I hired a woman."

Pierce's mouth fell open. "A woman! You hired a *woman* bodyguard?"

"Careful there," Gage murmured, but Pierce ignored him.

"Just what's wrong with a woman bodyguard?" Claire demanded.

"If I needed protection—which I'm not saying I do," Pierce said. "But if I needed protection, just how good do you think a woman would be at providing it?"

"This particular woman is highly qualified," Claire informed him. "She was an MP in the marines for four years. The last eight months of which were spent in the

Persian Gulf helping to keep the peace among who-knows-how-many battalions of homesick, horny soldiers."

"She ought to be able to handle Pierce, then," Gage said, aiming a sly grin at his brother.

Tara put her hand on her husband's knee, silently shushing him, and shook her head at her brother-in-law, quelling whatever response he had been about to make. "Listen to Claire," she ordered softly.

"She's also an expert pistol shot," Claire went on, regally ignoring the byplay, "and she has a black belt in karate. Bill Bender couldn't praise her enough," she added, referring to a former stuntman who'd been running a very successful and very discreet personal security business ever since he got too old and sore to fall out of buildings for a living. "He says she's as tough as they come."

"Oh, my God." Pierce moaned, falling against the back of the sofa as if he'd been shot. He covered his face with his hands. "You're siccing a female Rambo on me," he accused from behind his splayed fingers. "A no-neck ex-Marine sumo wrestler in a skirt and combat boots!"

"I'm providing you with some much-needed protection," Claire corrected calmly, ignoring his theatrics with the ease of long practice. "And if you refuse to cooperate with me, then I *will* sic a female Rambo on you." She smiled slightly as she played her trump card. "I'll call Mom home from Italy."

Pierce lowered his hands from in front of his face. "You wouldn't," he said, aghast at the very thought.

"I would."

"But she's *working*," he said, trying to appeal to his sister's overdeveloped work ethic. "The old man's running amok over there with his leading lady—"

"So?" Claire said, letting him know he wasn't going to distract her with that sorry old chestnut.

All four of them knew—all of *Hollywood* knew—that Elise Gage had stopped concerning herself with her ex-husband's affairs a good fifteen years ago, when she'd finally filed for their second divorce. The only time she paid any attention to his love life now was when it threatened to interfere with the smooth operation of Kingston Productions.

Which was exactly what Pierce was getting at.

"Now, don't look at me like that, Claire," he said. "It's no secret that Dad's latest romance is interfering with business. He's behind schedule and way over budget on *Mafioso*. Not to mention the scandal he's creating." He glanced over at his brother and sister-in-law to solicit their support, seeming to have suddenly forgotten that he'd been the focus of more than one scandal himself. "Francesca Soleri is only twenty," he told them, feigning shocked dismay at his father's outrageous behavior, "and I read somewhere that she'd been living in a convent before Dad discovered her."

"Oh, please." Claire rolled her eyes. "She's twenty-three going on thirty-five and the closest she's ever been to a convent is driving by one on the way to some illicit assignation."

"Well, you know how the Italian paparazzi are," Pierce said, undeterred by the soundness of her argument. "Much worse than the American press when they get their teeth into a story. No telling how much damage has already been done." He looked up at his sister with an expression of extreme reasonableness. "You wouldn't want to call Mom home before she's got everything straightened out over there, would you?" he asked, gifting her with his most sincere and sweetly persuasive smile, the one that never failed to get him what he wanted from most women. "Think what it could do to the bottom line."

He'd forgotten that Claire wasn't most women. She was his sister, comfortably familiar with his devastating charm. And she'd been an actress herself not so many years ago—one of the most accomplished child stars in the business before she'd decided she preferred working behind the cameras. She sat down next to her brother and put her hand on his arm.

"Do you really think the bottom line is more important to Mom—to *me*—than your safety?" she asked softly, lifting her gaze to his as she spoke. Her eyes were the same piercing blue as his own, the irises large and jewel bright beneath a film of unshed tears.

"Aw, jeez, Claire. That's not fair."

His sister's lower lip quivered pathetically.

"You're unscrupulous, you know that?" He threw her hand off his arm, pretending disgust. "Totally unscrupulous."

She blinked, allowing a single tear to well up over her bottom eyelid. It hung, suspended like a tiny diamond, in the web of her dark lashes.

"You might as well give up, Pierce," Gage advised, grinning as he watched his siblings try to outact each other. "She's got you."

"But I don't want a damn bodygu—"

Claire blinked again, dislodging the tear.

"Oh, all right. All right." Pierce threw his hands up, knowing he was beaten. He'd never been able to sit by and watch his baby sister cry. Even when he knew she was faking it. "I surrender. You win. I'll do whatever you want. I'll let this GI Jane of yours follow me around. Hell, I'll let a whole battalion of them follow me around if it'll make you happy. Just stop looking at me like I've dismembered your favorite doll."

The threatened tears dried up as if by magic. "I'm just asking you to meet her," she said, gracious in victory. "Just talk to her. If you don't like her we'll get someone else."

"Yeah, right," Pierce said, knowing his sister better than that. He reached out and lifted her chin with his index finger. "You've still got the touch, kid," he said admiringly, using his thumb to wipe away the single tear that had rolled down her ivory cheek.

2

NIKKI MARTINELLI stood in front of the mirror that hung on the back of her bedroom door and decided that, no, the faded blue jeans and meticulously polished Bass loafers weren't going to do it, after all. Even dressed up with a tailored white blouse and the boxy red linen jacket from her one and only suit, they still looked woefully unprofessional. Too casual and breezy. Too...

She tilted her head, studying her reflection with the critical eye of a woman who'd learned that appearances counted in La La Land. Usually a lot more than they should.

Too unremittingly preppy, she finally decided. She looked like an overindulged U.C.L.A. coed out to spend as much of her daddy's money as possible in the ritzy stores on Rodeo Drive.

Not exactly the image she'd been aiming for.

Nor one Claire Kingston would likely be willing to pay for.

According to Bill Bender, Hollywood's most beautiful producer had made it abundantly clear she was intent on hiring some serious muscle to protect her pretty-boy movie-star brother from a crazy letter-writing fan.

And serious muscle, Nikki knew, demanded seriously muscular clothes. Especially in Hollywood, where people were frequently judged by how closely they resembled the overwrought fantasies brought to life on movie screens all over the world.

Unfortunately, the only thing the least bit serious about the outfit she had on was the 9mm Baretta automatic tucked, out of sight beneath the red jacket, in the shoulder holster under her left arm.

She glanced into her open closet, wondering if showing up at Pierce Kingston's Beverly Hills estate in full military regalia, complete with combat boots, helmet, sidearm and nightstick would be considered sufficiently serious by her prospective employers.

"Naw," she said aloud, grimacing at her reflection in the mirror. They'd probably think she'd stopped by on her way over to audition for a part as a commando in the new movie about neo-Nazis being cast over at Universal.

Besides, even though Claire Kingston had made it clear she wanted to hire some serious muscle, she'd been equally adamant that it be female muscle. Apparently, protecting her brother's reputation as a macho leading man was at least as important as protecting the man himself. Pierce Kingston had a new movie coming out soon—one of those action-adventure epics full of guts and glory, bold heroics and impossible feats of derring-do. It might hurt the box office if people got the idea that the hero of such a movie was incapable of protecting himself. Which meant that having a marine in combat fatigues—female or otherwise—trailing around after him to see that he didn't get himself hurt by a pen-wielding, lovesick fan would no doubt be frowned upon by the entire Kingston clan.

Suppressing a sigh, Nikki toed off her loafers and wriggled out of her jeans, mentally reviewing the meager contents of her wardrobe. What she needed, she decided, was something that would make her look competent and tough but not butch. Sort of *L.A. Law*'s Grace Van Owen meets Sarah Connor from *Terminator 2*.

There was really only one item of clothing that would do all that, she thought, and reached into the closet for the black leather pants she'd just recently spent three months of her clothing budget on.

GEARING DOWN as she approached the driveway to Pierce Kingston's swanky estate, Nikki wondered— again—if riding her Harley Sportster to what was essentially a job interview had been a sound business decision.

Not that she'd really had any other choice. The ancient VW Bug she'd bought after mustering out of the marines was in the shop again, so the Harley was her only means of transportation unless she wanted to spring for a taxi. Which she didn't. Taxis were an expensive luxury and they often left one stranded at the mercy of others; Nikki didn't believe in wasting time or money. Especially when she had the Harley.

And, what the hell, she thought, grinning at herself in the side mirror as she leaned into the long curving driveway, *it goes with the leather pants.*

Of course, those might have been a mistake, too. One that might not be completely mitigated by the fact that she'd tried to tone down their impact by teaming them with her red blazer rather than wearing the more practical black motorcycle jacket she usually wore for riding. But whatever their impact, she thought, shrugging, it was way too late to change now.

Refusing to think anymore about it—or about why she'd suddenly reverted to her old adolescent pattern of worrying about making the right impression—Nikki brought the Harley to a smooth stop behind the rear fender of a low-slung silver Jaguar and shoved the Harley's kickstand into place with her foot.

Parked next to the Jag was a pale yellow Mercedes station wagon with a top-of-the-line baby seat visible through the back window. Three other vehicles, a flashy red Lamborghini, a gleaming black four-wheel-drive Range Rover and—that requisite for true Hollywood stardom—a Rolls-Royce limousine, were visible in the open bays of the five-car garage.

With a low whistle of admiration, Nikki tugged off her helmet and looked around.

A whimsical English topiary garden with fragrant rose bushes and evergreen shrubs sculpted into fanciful shapes surrounded a small neoclassical fountain, which sat directly in front of the house, creating a roundabout driveway for easy in-and-out access. Lush velvet lawns bordered the wide curving driveway, sloping off to the left to the perfectly manicured man-high hedges that protected the tennis courts and cabana and hid the swimming pool from view. Stately evergreen trees, tall pink dogwoods in full bloom and bright beds of well-tended flowers surrounded the huge Norman English "castle," framing it like a rare and expensive painting. A pair of stone lions reclined in bored and regal splendor on either side of the massive double-wide front door.

Nikki eyed them, wondering if they'd been put there in Louis B. Mayer's time as a sly tongue-in-cheek reference to the MGM mascot—Hollywood legend had it that one of his mistresses used to live in the house.

"Welcome to the world of the rich and famous," Nikki muttered to herself as she swung her leg over the saddle of the bike and stood up.

She was bent over, peering into the side mirror, her helmet dangling from one hand, finger-fluffing her hair with the other, when she heard the front door open. She looked up quickly, the beginnings of a warm smile of greeting turning up her generous mouth at the corners.

A small, dark-haired woman in a simple blue dress with a plain white bibbed apron tied over it stood in the wide doorway, staring down at her with a stern expression on her face. "Miss Martinelli?" she inquired.

Nikki's smile faltered and she nodded, suddenly feeling as if she were back at boot camp about to be chewed out by a superior officer for something she hadn't even realized she'd done. "I was just making a few quick repairs," she said, gesturing toward the mirror.

"Indeed," the woman replied briskly, sounding like a cross between Mary Poppins and a drill sergeant.

Nikki wondered if it was her or the Harley. *Probably both*, she thought sourly, knowing what most people expected from a woman who rode a "hog."

"I'm Marjorie Gilmore. Mr. Kingston's housekeeper. I heard your motorcycle when you came up the drive," she said, giving Nikki the distinct impression that the noise had been unnecessarily excessive. "Won't you come in, please?" She stepped back from the doorway. "We've been expecting you."

And you're late.

Marjorie Gilmore didn't say the words but Nikki definitely heard them. She glanced at her watch, checking to see if the unspoken accusation was true. She was gratified to see that it wasn't; like anyone who'd grown up in a military household, she had a keen appreciation of the value of time and abhorred wasting it. Hers or anyone else's.

"Miss Martinelli?" the housekeeper prompted, making Nikki realize she was dawdling.

Not wanting to keep the woman waiting while she strapped her helmet to the Harley, Nikki tucked it under her arm and mounted the wide, smooth stone steps. "Ma'am," she said, suppressing the urge to salute as she moved past the woman and into the house.

The door shut behind her with a sharp click. "This way," Marjorie Gilmore said, and turned to lead the way across the polished black-and-white marble of the huge foyer and down a long carpeted hallway that led off into the depths of the house.

Nice, Nikki thought, her gaze darting from side to side as she followed the housekeeper. She gathered quick impressions of light and color and quiet good taste without any of the ostentatiousness the magnificence on the outside had led her to expect. And then the housekeeper stopped and stepped aside, ushering Nikki through the doorway ahead of her.

"Miss Martinelli has arrived," she said, and melted back into the hall. The word *finally* hovered, unspoken, in the air behind her.

"Thank you, ma'am," Nikki said to her back, determined to out-polite the woman if nothing else. And then she turned smartly, in her best parade-ground style, to face the people gathered on the other side of the room.

Her first, unedited thought was that they were the most beautiful group of people she'd ever seen—which was saying a lot in an environment where beauty was a prerequisite for success and even coffee-shop waitresses were expected to be gorgeous. Viewed singularly, any one of them was enough to merit a long second look of awe and admiration. Viewed as a group they were almost—Nikki struggled to find the right word. *Overwhelming*, was the only one she could come up with.

An all-too-familiar sense of inadequacy came stealing over her as she stood there staring at them. It had been a long time since she'd felt like the geeky new kid on the base, all arms and legs and tongue-tied adolescent awkwardness at being confronted by the members of the in-group. It was a feeling she remembered all too well. And the big, blond Adonis lounging on the chintz sofa with such elegant, self-confident ease—the living embodiment of every high school quarterback who'd never noticed her—didn't help her flagging self-confidence one tiny bit.

He was long and lean, half-reclining on the plump seat of the oversized sofa like some spoiled Eastern potentate at leisure in his harem. His clothes were dark and dramatic, intensifying the aura of indolent ease and providing a perfect foil for his golden good looks. Slim black jeans sheathed his long legs and narrow hips. A loose silky black shirt adorned his upper body. The finely textured sericeous fabric caressed his muscled torso like fond feminine hands; the dropped-shoulder styling of the yoke emphasized his impressively broad shoulders; the open collar showed a tasteful, tantalizing glimpse of curling chest hair; the rolled back cuffs revealed the strength of his forearms and the pure masculine beauty of his long-fingered hands.

His blond hair was thick and softly curling, touching the collar of his black shirt, framing a face that would have made Michelangelo weep with despair at the impossibility of ever doing it justice in mere marble. His brow was noble; his nose was strong and aristocratic; his jaw and chin were sheer chiseled perfection; his finely molded lips were the stuff of a million female fantasies. But it was his eyes—those world-famous, mesmerizing, penetrating eyes—that really caught and held Nikki's fascinated attention. They were the brightest, bluest, most deliciously *wicked* eyes she'd ever seen.

And they were staring straight into hers.

Nikki swallowed, trying to bring some moisture to her suddenly dry mouth. What had happened, she wondered with fast growing alarm, to all her hard-won self-confidence? To the brash, bold, in-your-face cockiness with which she'd learned to stare down the world? What had happened to the woman who had vowed—*vowed!*—to never, ever let herself be swayed by the mere sight of a pretty face again?

GOOD GOD, Pierce thought and slowly straightened to a full upright position on the sofa. An Amazon goddess had just entered his garden room wearing handtooled cowboy boots and skintight, black leather pants that hugged every inch of the longest, leanest, shapeliest legs he'd ever been privileged to see. She had a black motorcycle helmet tucked under her right arm, reminding him of a knight about to arm for battle, and her booted feet were planted slightly apart on the terrazzo tiles. Her back was ramrod straight, her head up, her chest out, like a soldier ready and waiting for orders.

Pierce immediately thought of several very intimate orders he'd like to give her as his gaze traveled upward over the fantasy-inspiring length of her legs.

The rest of her was as slim and gorgeous as her fabulous legs, narrow where a woman should be narrow, curved—as far as he could tell under the loose red jacket—where a woman should curve. Her hair was black and shiny, cut in one of those supershort styles that should have made her look boyish but most emphatically didn't. The tousled, feathery layers framed a face of fierce and vivid beauty. Her eyes were the pale green of fine peridots, bold and uncompromising beneath the straight slash of her unadorned brows as she returned his stare; her cheekbones were high and exquisitely chiseled; her nose was narrow; her mouth was wide and generous, as inviting as carnal sin, beneath a light coating of clear lip gloss.

Pierce grinned slowly, in frank admiration and masculine appreciation, and was rewarded by the slow bloom of color in her cheeks. *Maybe having a bodyguard won't be so bad, after all*, he thought, wondering if he could get her to turn around so he could see how those black leather pants looked from the back.

And then someone kicked him in the ankle—his brother, he realized, scowling—and he tore his gaze away from the goddess's face to find that everyone else had already come to their feet. Claire was, in fact, already halfway across the room.

"Ms. Martinelli," she said, her hand extended in greeting. "It's a pleasure to finally meet you."

Nikki juggled her motorcycle helmet from one arm to the other to shake hands, inadvertently exposing the butt of the gun under her left arm. She covered it back up with a quick yank on the front of her jacket and stuck out her hand. "Thank you. It's a pleasure to, ah...meet..." Her eyes darted from Claire's face to Pierce's and back again, like a child sneaking peeks at the beribboned birthday gift she wasn't allowed to open until all the proper amenities had been observed.

Snap out of it! she ordered herself, when she realized what she was doing. Pierce Kingston wasn't the only—or even the most—good-looking man in Hollywood. And, even if he was, well...she'd sworn off men like him over four years ago, after the fiasco of her engagement to another man who was better looking than a man had any right to be. Nikki straightened her already straight shoulders, deliberately blocking Pierce Kingston's gorgeous face from her mind by focusing on his sister's.

"It's a pleasure to meet you, too, Ms. Kingston," she said briskly, forcing herself to deal with the matter at hand.

"Call me Claire, please," Claire said kindly, fully aware of the effect her brother had on the opposite sex—even when he *wasn't* deliberately sending out signals like a heat-seeking missile. "And I'll call you Nikki, shall I?" she said, drawing her guest across the room with her as she spoke. "Is that short for anything?"

"No, it's just Nikki," Nikki said. "It was supposed to be Nicholas but I surprised my dad."

"Hoping for a son after a string of daughters?" Tara asked pleasantly.

Nikki shook her head. "Hoping for another boy to complete the family basketball team," she said without a trace of the rancor her status in the family had caused during most of her teenage years. "I saw you last year in *The Promise*, Miss Channing," she blurted out like a star-struck teenager. "You were wonderful."

How about me? Pierce wondered sourly, piqued that she seemed to be deliberately ignoring him. *Wasn't I wonderful, too?* He had, after all, gotten an Oscar nomination for his role in the movie.

"Thank you," Tara said graciously. "But it's just plain Tara, please."

"You couldn't be plain if you tried, sweetheart," Gage said to his wife as he reached around her to offer his hand to Nikki. "I'm just plain Gage, though," he said, introducing himself.

"Not so plain," Nikki said as she shook his hand. "You won an Oscar for the cinematography on *The Promise*. Your third, I think."

"Yes." Gage smiled, pleased and impressed. Most people not in the business didn't even know what a cinematographer was. "How did you know that?"

"Bill briefed me," Nikki admitted.

"And this," Claire said, gesturing toward Pierce, "is Pierce. He's—"

"The body you're going to be guarding," Pierce interrupted smoothly, coming to his feet as he spoke. He reached out and took Nikki's hand in his, holding it in a grip that was somehow more intimate than that used for merely shaking hands. "I'm looking forward to having you shadow my every move," he said, smiling into eyes that were almost on a level with his. *Good God,* he thought, intrigued, *she must be nearly six feet tall.* He glanced down for just a second, running his gaze once again over the length of her leather-clad legs. They went on for miles, endless, inspiring and perfectly, outrageously gorgeous. A little thrill of excitement raced through him as half-a-dozen lascivious pictures formed in his highly inventive mind. Long, smooth thighs clasping his hips. Rounded kneecaps, bent and dimpled, draped over his shoulders. Trim ankles locked together in the small of his back. He looked up then, after that split second of speculation, his unspoken thoughts as clear to her as if he'd described each heated fantasy in intimate detail.

Nikki stared back at him, mesmerized, unable to look away, her expression half shocked, half intrigued and wholly, helplessly fascinated.

He smiled like a pirate bent on plundering her treasures, the rakish look in his eyes promising untold treasures in return.

Nikki gasped softly, indignantly, and tore her gaze away at last, trying, belatedly, to take her hand out of his.

Pierce smiled, refusing to release her, and drew her hand to within a scant millimeter of his lips. "I predict a long and blissful—" he waited until she'd lifted her lashes and locked her gaze with his again "—association," he said blandly, although the look in his eyes was anything but.

They stared at each other for another heartbeat's worth of time that seemed aeons long. Heat met heat. Challenge met challenge. A silent proclamation of amorous intent was declared by a pair of laser blue eyes. And furiously denied in the gleam of clear green ones. And then Pierce smiled again, slowly, in anticipation and delight and deliberate provocation, and touched his lips to the back of her hand.

"Oh, for heaven's sake, Pierce," said his sister. Exasperation warred with reluctant admiration in her voice. "Quit showing off and behave yourself. We have business to discuss."

"GIRLFRIEND?" Nikki said a few moments later, trying not to look as alarmed as she felt at the prospect the Kingstons had just laid before her. "Bill Bender didn't say anything about pretending to be anybody's girl-friend. Especially not anybody's live-in girlfriend," she added, appalled at the very idea. She glanced around at the four of them, one by one, her expression rife with the suspicion that she was somehow being railroaded.

Tara Channing-Kingston gazed back at her out of slanted aquamarine eyes, looking sincere and concerned and not the least bit conniving. Gage Kingston's expression was decidedly amused. Claire was poised and expectant, the epitome of executive calm and confidence. And Pierce, once again lounging on the sofa across from her, looked like a hungry cat who had every expectation of being given the keys to an aviary. Nikki bit her lower lip, refusing to acknowledge the erratic jump of her pulse as she met his eyes, and shifted her gaze back to Claire's face.

"Bill said you were looking for a bodyguard who could be discreet," she said, careful not to look at Pierce again. "Someone who could blend into the background and not be noticed."

"Maybe with a bag over your head," Pierce muttered.

Gage snickered.

"And wearing a floor length gunnysack," Pierce added.

Tara frowned and shushed them both.

Claire shot a warning glance at Pierce, silently telling him to keep out of this and let her handle it. "What Bill meant was," she said, smiling her producer smile at Nikki, "that we need someone who can blend in *here.*" She lifted a graceful hand in a gesture that encompassed more than just the lovely room in which they all sat. "In Beverly Hills and at Hollywood parties and . . . things like that. I'm sure you understand," she said confidingly. "What we want is someone whose appearance doesn't scream 'bodyguard.' Especially to anyone connected with the press."

Nikki nodded. *Of course*, she reminded herself, mentally hitting the heel of her hand to her forehead, *I knew that*. "Bill said you didn't want anyone knowing you'd hired a bodyguard because of the new movie coming out. And I've certainly been in Hollywood long enough to understand the reasoning behind that decision. But is it really necessary to pretend I'm his—" she cast a quick, nervous glance at Pierce out of the corners of her eyes "—latest . . ." She floundered, searching for any word other than the one that had sprung instantly to mind when she looked at him. "His latest . . ."

"Lover," Pierce supplied helpfully.

Nikki forgot herself long enough to glare at him.

He smiled back at her, his expression bland and innocent. And full of wicked speculation.

Nikki hurriedly turned her gaze back to Claire. "Wouldn't it be just as effective," she continued, trying to pretend Pierce Kingston wasn't even on the same planet, let alone in the same room with her, "if I pretended to be his—oh, I don't know—his secretary or something?"

"I already have a secretary," Pierce said, as if she'd addressed the question to him. "Kathy Frye. Great secretary," he added musingly. "She's been with me for—what?" He glanced at his sister. "A year, now?"

"Just about," Claire said.

"She's been with me for a year, and she's probably the best secretary I've ever had," he said to Nikki. "I couldn't fire her just to provide you with a cover. Besides—" he grinned again, triumphantly "—she doesn't live in. Stays over once in a while if she's had to work late," he admitted with a shrug, "but she doesn't live in."

"I could pose as a new maid," Nikki said to Claire, knowing, even as she said it, that she was clutching at straws. "A maid would live in, wouldn't she?"

"I don't have a maid," Pierce said. "A service comes in once a week to help Mrs. Gilmore with the heavy cleaning. Sometimes her niece helps out, too, if there's something special going on."

Exasperated, Nikki finally looked directly at him. "Well, you could *hire* a maid, couldn't you?"

Pierce shook his head. "Mrs. Gilmore wouldn't like it."

No, Nikki thought, as a picture of the formidable little woman formed in her mind, *I don't imagine she would*. "And is Mrs. Gilmore the one in charge of things around here?"

"As a matter of fact, she is," Pierce said mildly, refusing to take offense at the implied challenge to his authority. "Nothing would get done around here if it wasn't for her."

"I can believe that," Nikki began.

"Having you pose as a maid really wouldn't do us any good, anyway," Claire interrupted smoothly, steering the conversation back in the direction she wanted it to go before things got out of hand. "We need someone who can accompany Pierce everywhere he goes without arousing any speculation or suspicion. A maid couldn't do that."

"No, of course not," Nikki conceded. "I should have thought of that myself." And she would have, too, if Pierce Kingston's laserlike stare hadn't rattled her to her bones. "But having me pretend to be his new girlfriend—" she refused to say 'lover' "—is going to raise all kinds of speculation."

"Speculation, yes," Claire agreed. "But not suspicion."

"But if I pose as his assistant, maybe some kind of glorified gofer or something, that would eliminate the suspicion *and* the speculation."

Gage chuckled. "Maybe if you wore a bag over your head," he said, quoting his brother's earlier remark.

Nikki looked up at him, a request for clarification in her clear green eyes.

"What my husband is trying to say," Tara explained, "is that you're a very attractive woman and, even if you really were Pierce's assistant, no one would ever believe that's *all* you were to him."

Nikki considered that. "Because of his playboy reputation, you mean?" she said, nodding toward Pierce.

"Well, there is that, of course." Tara flashed a teasing smile at her brother-in-law. "But I was thinking more of the Hollywood gossip mill than anything else," she said seriously, speaking as a woman who'd spent her entire career surrounded by whispers and innuendo. "It's always voracious and can be vicious, as well."

Nikki nodded her understanding—and her acceptance. "Okay," she said, looking at Claire. "How do you want to set this up?"

"Shouldn't you be asking *me* that question?" Pierce asked.

Nikki continued to look at Claire. "I thought you were the one who was hiring me."

"Actually, no. Kingston Productions is hiring you. I only made the arrangements. And since it's Pierce's body you'll be guarding," she said slanting a teasing smile at her brother, "I guess he should have *some* say in things."

"Thank you so much," Pierce drawled. He came out of his casual slouch and slid forward on the sofa, prepared to take charge of the situation now that the preliminaries were over. It was time this long-legged Amazon learned just exactly who she was dealing with. "As Claire's already said," he began, "you'll live in and—" He broke off, looking over her shoulder at the woman in the doorway. "Yes, Mrs. Gilmore? What is it?"

"I'm sorry to interrupt, sir," she said briskly, "but the baby is awake and fussing. Mrs. Kingston asked me to let her know."

"Thank you, Mrs. Gilmore. I'll be right there," Tara said as she stood up. "Beau has a bit of a cold," she explained to no one in particular as she edged around the coffee table to follow the housekeeper. "It's been making him miserable."

"And everyone else within earshot," her husband added, coming to his feet beside his wife as he spoke. She looked up at him questioningly. "It's time we were leaving, anyway," he said, slipping his hand under Tara's elbow to keep her by his side while he made his goodbyes. "Pleasure to meet you, Nikki," he said, nodding at his brother's new bodyguard. His amber eyes gleamed with amusement. "I wish you luck with him." He transferred his gaze to his brother. "Try not to be too big a pain in the ass," he ordered gruffly. "Claire" he said, bending to kiss his sister's cheek. "See you at the studio tomorrow."

"I've got to be going, too," Claire said, standing up to join the general exodus. "I've got a meeting with Sly Stallone about that *Glory Days* script. We're having lunch at Le Dome." She glanced back and forth between her brother and Nikki. "Don't murder each other," she said, only half-teasing. "And let me know what arrangements you make."

And then, suddenly, just like that, there were only two people in the sunny, plant-filled garden room of Pierce Kingston's plush Beverly Hills estate. Five tense, silent seconds ticked by on an unseen clock. And then Nikki steeled her spine and turned her head to look across the coffee table at her new employer.

Pierce gave her his most roguish smile, the one that caused good girls to swoon in fearful excitement and bad girls to shiver in delicious anticipation of imminent ravishment. It started in his eyes, crinkling them up at the corners, and moved downward, causing his finely molded lips to turn upward in a slow, teasing grin that somehow managed to combine boyish innocence with the indecent, decadent intentions of an experienced rakehell.

Nikki narrowed her eyes at him. "You might as well save that movie-star smile for someone who's susceptible to it," she said. She used the uninterested, seen-it-all tone of voice that had always worked so well with hotshot jet jockeys intent on putting another notch on their throttles, and amorous GIs who wanted something exciting to write home about. "I'm not the least bit impressed," she added, trying to sound bored.

She wondered if he could tell she was lying.

3

NIKKI SPENT THE REST of the afternoon trying very hard
not to be impressed as her new employer showed her
around his palatial Beverly Hills estate, but it was a
nearly impossible task. Everything she saw impressed
her right down to the toes of her cowboy boots. The
house was one of the most beautiful she'd ever been inside, warm and cozy and quietly grand, despite the
overdone theatricality of the castlelike exterior. It was
full of cheerful English chintzes, fine-grained leather,
polished wood, luxuriantly healthy houseplants, and
more priceless works of art than Nikki had ever seen
outside of a museum.

The grounds were a marvel of the gardener's skills.
A perfect mix of fragrant, fecund growth and precision
grooming surrounded the sparkling blue pool, hot tub
and cabana area before spreading out in a lush emerald
carpet to encompass the tennis court beyond.

And the man—ah, the man!—was the most fascinating, the most effortlessly charming, the most splendidly male animal she'd ever run into in her life.

And she'd grown up in a house full of splendid men
who had enough charm between them to turn Queen
Elizabeth of England into a flustered, giggling schoolgirl.

"So just treat him like one of your brothers," Nikki
mumbled to herself as she followed her host up the wide
curving staircase to the second floor.

"Beg pardon?" Pierce asked, his large, elegant hand unconsciously caressing the polished black walnut railing as he turned back to look at her.

"I, ah . . . asked if that was a Picasso," she said, gesturing toward the painting at the top of the stairs. It depicted a woman with one eye, two noses and three breasts, with skin a color no real woman had ever had. Unless, Nikki thought whimsically, the poor thing had been standing naked out in the snow for a couple of hours.

Pierce nodded. "From his blue period," he said. "It's not really to my taste," he added, grimacing at it over his shoulder as they passed it. "But Claire said it was a good investment. And I always listen to Claire when it comes to making investments."

They passed a few more pieces of artwork as they moved down the hall—a delicate art deco sculpture displayed under glass on a narrow marble column, a colorful abstract with an Oriental feeling and a bold silk screen done in a style that looked vaguely familiar.

"Are these wired?" Nikki asked, leaning down a bit to peer at the signature on the silk screen. It was an Andy Warhol.

"Wired?"

"With an alarm," she clarified. "They're just—" she waved a hand at the wall "—hanging there. Don't you worry about someone waltzing in here and walking off with one?"

Pierce shook his head. "Try to take one off the wall and all hell breaks loose. Sirens. Lights. The whole nine yards."

Nikki leaned a little closer, carefully inspecting the edges of the frame for wires or sensors. None were visible. "What kind of system is it?"

Pierce shrugged. "I haven't the foggiest idea," he said. "Claire had it installed after I bought this place." He paused and pushed open a door. "Here's your room." He stood back to usher her in ahead of him.

Nikki sidled past him, careful not to brush up against his splendid body, and stepped into the room. The decor was quaint, comfortable and quietly wealthy, calling up visions of country weekends at English manor houses. The flowing drapes on the tall, multipaned windows, the thick, puffy bedspread with its matching pillow shams, and one of the wing chairs in front of the fireplace were all done in a Laura Ashley-type print overrun with rambling ivy in soft shades of green on a pale ivory background. The rest of the room was done in spruce green and cream with touches of faded rose. The whole thing was bigger than her entire apartment. And the bed was absolutely, decadently huge.

Nikki turned away from it to admire the misty Impressionist painting hanging over the fireplace. It depicted three Edwardian ladies in various stages of dishabille cavorting by a stream. "Lovely," she said, determined not to enthuse all over her host.

"The bathroom's through there." Pierce nodded toward a half-open door and Nikki peered in, catching a glimpse of thick dark green towels and gleaming rose-colored tile. "You've got it all to yourself," he said. "So you don't have to worry about hogging the tub."

"I prefer showers."

"Well, there's one of those, too. But you really ought to give the tub a try while you're here. It has massage jets." He lifted his arm to push the door further open, moving forward as if he meant to point them out to her.

Nikki backed against the door frame, instinctively retreating from the zing of awareness that shot through her at his nearness.

"Most women find massage jets very—" he paused, smiling wolfishly to let her know he was aware of what she'd done—and why she'd done it "—relaxing," he finished with a suggestive lift of his eyebrow.

"Mmm-hmm," Nikki said, sidestepping the remark—and him. She turned toward the windows. "It's a lovely view from in here."

Pierce stared at her ramrod-straight back for a moment, wondering what she'd do if he put his hands on her shoulders and steered her toward the bed. He decided it was too soon to find out. *Maybe tomorrow,* he thought. He'd give her a day to get used to him before he jumped her gorgeous bones. "It's even lovelier from outside," he said.

He moved around her and lifted the latch on one of the long windows, pulling them inward.

"Oh, it's a door." Nikki hurried past him, trying not to run in her eagerness to be out of the bedroom, and stepped through the glass doors and onto a wide stone terrace overlooking the grounds. It was topped by an ivy and bougainvillea-draped balustrade like that at the top of a castle wall. A smooth stone staircase led down to the pool below. Nikki hurried to the rail and leaned over it to look down.

"You're right," she said when Pierce sauntered over to join her. "It is better from out here." She didn't turn her head as she spoke, preferring to let him think she was enthralled by the view of his backyard.

"Yes," Pierce said. He leaned an elbow on the wide stone balustrade and turned to face her, positioning himself just a little closer than he knew she'd be comfortable with but not so close that she could reasonably object.

Nikki tensed with instinctive feminine caution. She wanted to move away but didn't, deciding to hold her ground instead. She knew all the sneaky little stratagems men used to intimidate and impress women—having four older brothers gave a woman quite an eduction—and she knew the best way to counter that first, tentative come-on was to pretend she hadn't even noticed it. The male ego couldn't take being ignored.

"We must be right over the garden room up here," she said, as if architecture were the only thing on her mind.

"You've got a good sense of direction," Pierce complimented her. "I'd lived in this pile of stones a couple of weeks before I figured that out." His wide shoulders lifted in a self-deprecating shrug. "I still get lost sometimes," he confided, leaning just a tiny bit closer to her.

Nikki continued to hold her ground; she didn't move but she didn't look at him, either. "It's a big house," she agreed, her gaze glued to the bright red flower she was fiddling with as she tried to think of something else to say to him. Something clever. Idle, inconsequential words were great for creating distance between people; strained silences were . . . unnerving.

Pierce let her fidget for another thirty seconds before letting her off the hook. "I have breakfast out here nearly every morning when I'm home," he said easily, wondering if her hair was as fine and silky as it looked. Wondering, too, what she'd do if he reached out and touched it. Then, never having been one to deny himself anything he wanted—never having *been* denied—he decided to find out. "You're welcome to join me whenever you like," he said, reaching out to tuck a feathery wisp of hair behind her ear as he spoke.

She looked up quickly, uncertainly, her eyes darting to his in alarm and warning, but he'd already taken his hand away, robbing her of the need to tell him to keep his hands to himself.

She reached up with her own hand, nervously smoothing the place he'd touched. "Join you?" she said, because she couldn't think of anything else to say.

"For breakfast. Right there." He lifted his hand and gestured behind her at the wrought-iron, glass-topped table and chairs. "Every morning at eight-thirty unless I'm filming."

"Thank you, no," Nikki said politely. Virtuously. "I'm up much earlier than that."

"So am I."

"But you said—"

"I said I had breakfast at eighty-thirty. I get up at six."

"Oh?" It was the same time she usually woke up. She liked to get her daily workout over the first thing in the morning.

"I like to work out first thing in the morning." He nodded toward the pool. "Laps. Then weights. Then a round or two with the bags. There's a small gym in the cabana."

"You box?" Nikki asked, surprised into displaying her interest.

"Only with the bags."

Well, that explains the shoulders, Nikki thought, covertly admiring them out of the corner of her eye.

"Have you ever tried it?"

"What?"

"The bags."

Nikki shook her head.

"You ought to. Lots of women do, these days. It's a great workout."

"I can tell," she said, her gaze flitting over the width of his shoulders beneath the black silk before she could think to stop herself.

Pierce's eyes took on a predatory gleam. "You noticed, huh?"

Too late, Nikki realized what she'd revealed. "Different workouts develop different muscle groups," she said, trying to cover her lapse with a veneer of brisk professionalism. "You've obviously done a lot of work on your pecs and deltoids and . . ." Her voice trailed off at the heated look in his eyes.

"I like the muscle groups your workout has developed, too," he said teasingly, and lifted his hand to touch her.

Nikki stiffened and leveled a killing glance at him, the one she'd learned early stopped most men from going any further.

But Pierce Kingston wasn't most men. He'd been spoiled and indulged by women from the cradle, given what he wanted without ever having to ask for it, sure of his welcome. And, besides, he didn't intend to do anything more than test the strength of her biceps.

"Impressive," he said, squeezing it lightly through the sleeve of her jacket, letting her go before she could object. "But tense." His blue eyes flashed teasingly, imbuing his next words with a wealth of innuendo. "You ought to learn to relax."

Nikki's green eyes turned frosty. "And you've got just the thing for that, I suppose," she said, knowing what was coming next.

She was wrong.

"A few rounds with the body bag would loosen you right up," Pierce said. He knew what she'd been expecting him to say; he could see it in her eyes. He also

knew a man never got anywhere with a woman by doing what she expected him to. Disarm and conquer, that
was his motto. He gave her a friendly smile. "Why don't
we go downstairs and you can meet the staff?"

SHE MET THE GARDENER first, digging in a flower bed on
the far side of the cabana. She was in her mid-thirties
and California-girl pretty, with a wide smile and a trim
figure encased in faded jeans and a light blue T-shirt
with the words *flower power* emblazoned across the
chest. She was also divorced, Nikki learned. And she
looked at Pierce—when he wasn't looking at her—as if
she'd like to nibble him to death. Nikki made a mental
note that the gardener came in once a week and took
care of all the houseplants, as well as the gardens, giving her free access to the entire estate.

She met his secretary in her well-appointed first floor
office. "Nikki, this is Kathy Frye," Pierce said, his smile
all careless charm and flattery as he made the intro-
duction. "The best secretary a man ever had. Kathy, I'd
like you to meet Nikki Martinelli, my new bodyguard."

Nikki reached across the desk to shake hands with
the secretary. She was an attractive woman in her mid-
to-late forties, with gleaming auburn hair, dark ex-
pressive eyes and the figure of a woman who took pains
to keep herself in shape. She was meticulously
groomed, Nikki noted, her nails short but beautifully
manicured, her makeup skillfully applied to conceal all
evidence of crow's-feet or laugh lines. Her teal suit was
businesslike but feminine, and the scent of some expensive, exotic perfume lingered in the air around her.

"Bodyguard?" Kathy said, looking at Pierce.

He made a face. "The baby-blue letters," he explained. "Claire thinks I need protection."

Kathy Frye's forehead wrinkled. "You have that interview with *People* at three o'clock this afternoon," she warned him. "A writer and a photographer."

"Not to worry." Pierce dropped a brawny silk-clad arm around Nikki's shoulders and hugged her against his side. She fit him perfectly, he noted. "As far as the world is concerned, Ms. Martinelli is my latest squeeze." He dropped a light, nuzzling kiss on her temple. "Isn't that right, darling?"

"Right," Nikki said stiffly.

Kathy Frye laughed. "Well, either keep her out of sight or give her a few quick acting lessons," she advised. "She isn't going to fool anybody otherwise."

Pierce looked at the woman at his side. "I told you, you were too tense," he chided, looking pleased with himself. They found the housekeeper in the kitchen, fixing a tea tray for the afternoon's interview.

"You've already met Mrs. Gilmore," Pierce said, smiling at the woman who was standing at a butcher-block island near the gleaming double sink. She was cutting the crusts off bread with a very large, very sharp chef's knife. "The woman without whom this place would fall apart."

"Miss Martinelli," the housekeeper said, nodding her acknowledgment of the compliment without pausing in her work.

"And Lisbeth Greene," Pierce said, introducing the young woman who was sitting at the table, polishing silver. She was young, eighteen or nineteen at most, Nikki guessed, with straight, shoulder-length brown hair cut in a bouncy bob and big blue eyes. She cast a wary glance at Nikki from under her wispy, overlong bangs.

"Lisbeth is Mrs. Gilmore's niece," Pierce said. "Remember? I mentioned her earlier this afternoon?"

"Yes," Nikki said, watching the young woman's eyes light up with adoration at this sign that the great Pierce Kingston was actually aware of her existence. "You said she comes in to help Mrs. Gilmore sometimes."

"And just to visit, too," Lisbeth said, with a shy smile at Pierce. "Sometimes."

"Anytime at all," Pierce said, casually reaching out to pat her hand before he reached for one of the fresh-baked scones already arranged on a silver tray on the counter. His housekeeper frowned at him from under her brows. He grinned and snatched one anyway, devouring half of it in one bite. Then, with a wink at the giggling Lisbeth, he took Nikki's hand in his and dragged her out of the kitchen.

"Let's go get you loosened up before that photographer gets here," he said, and popped the other half of the raisin-studded scone into her mouth before she could answer.

PIERCE'S IDEA of loosening her up consisted mostly of trying to convince her to remove her jacket and shoulder holster in order to make herself more comfortable. "I doubt I'm in any danger in my own house," he said reasonably when Nikki balked. "And what if the photographer from *People* sees the gun under your arm? That'd blow the lid off our cover story before we even get started." He assumed a serious, concerned expression. "Claire would have a fit if that happened."

"I don't intend for the photographer to see me at all," Nikki retorted. "So there's no way he's going to see my gun."

"You mean you're planning to leave me alone with them when they get here?" He gave her a scandalized look. "Unprotected?"

Nikki narrowed her eyes at him. "I thought you weren't in any danger in your own house."

"With people I know, sure," Pierce said, shameless in his attempt to get his own way. "But I've never met this reporter from *People.* Or the photographer. Either one of them could be a sex-crazed maniac who's after my body."

"If either one of them is female, I'm sure that's true," Nikki muttered to herself.

"What was that?"

"I said, I'm sure you've had lots of experience handling sex-crazed maniacs."

"Some," he admitted modestly, and then spoiled the effect by grinning his pirate's grin at her. "Want me to show you what experience has taught me?"

"No, thank you," Nikki said primly. "I'm not interested."

Pierce thought about letting that pass—for about two seconds. He was too much the dominant male animal to let a challenge like that go unanswered. "I could prove you wrong," he said silkily, moving toward her like a sleek jungle cat advancing on his prey.

Nikki trembled inwardly but held her ground, knowing she had to set some boundaries—now—before he got even more outrageous. "You could try," she said calmly. "But I wouldn't advise it."

Pierce moved closer, deliberately trying to make her break and run. "No?"

"No," she said firmly, not budging an inch.

They were practically nose to nose now, almost chest to breast, only a deep breath away from touching. "Who's gonna stop me?" he taunted.

Nikki didn't hesitate. "I am," she said, without taking her eyes from his.

He smiled wickedly. "You can try," he said, all but inviting her to do so. Hoping she would. "But you'd lose." He put his hands on her upper arms, his long fingers wrapping around her slender biceps, and felt her shiver. His eyes glittered with triumph. "You're going to like losing," he promised, and bent his head to kiss her.

Nikki pulled her head back a fraction of an inch. Just that, a small movement, a mere tensing of her neck muscles, a slight narrowing of her eyes as she stared at him, but it stopped him. For the moment. "It might interest you to know," she said coolly, in a tone that had caused more than one solider to back down from a confrontation, "that I know several very effective ways of disabling a man."

He grinned at the threat implied in her deceptively casual tone. "Do you?" he asked, as if inviting her to elaborate.

"Most of them are very painful. Or so I've been told." She lifted a mocking eyebrow, knowing its intimidation value from past experience. "I wouldn't want to hurt you but—"

"You will if you have to," he finished for her.

"Yes. I'm glad you understand me."

"Oh, I understand you, sweetheart," he said. "I understand you completely." And then he bent his head again and took her mouth with his.

Shock held her stock-still for a long, delicious moment. Shock that he would do such a thing after what
she'd just said to him. Shock that he *dared* when other
men had not. And then the heat of his mouth got
through to her, his casual expertise and unmistakable,
instinctive carnality touching a deeply buried nerve,
and she felt herself begin to respond. Her skin began to
tingle where he touched her. Her breasts began to
pucker and ache. Her lips began to part, opening for his
tongue. Panicked, she slid her booted foot behind his
bare ankle and pushed against his chest with both
hands.

He went down like a running back who'd been sandwiched between two opposing players coming from
opposite directions.

"I told you not to—" Nikki began hotly, and then she
shrieked as he scissored his feet around her legs and
brought her tumbling down to join him on the floor.
She felt his arms lock around her, pinning hers to her
sides as he rolled over on top of her.

Nikki struggled with restrained ferocity, trying to free
her arms or wind her leg around his to flip him, but he
blocked her every move with insulting ease, silently
informing her that the martial arts moves he displayed
on the movie screen weren't all for show. She cursed
and struggled a little harder.

"Is that the best you can do?" he inquired politely, his
eyes twinkling with amusement—and arousal.

Nikki glared at him. "If I wasn't afraid of doing some
permanent damage to that million-dollar hide of
yours," she hissed, trying a few moves designed to twist
her body out from underneath his, "I'd show you what
I can do."

"Twelve-million-dollar hide," he corrected her with a grin. *God, her body feels good*, he thought, as she squirmed beneath him. *Soft and warm. And strong*. It was all he could do to hold her without hurting either of them. "They paid me twelve million dollars for my last movie. Plus a percentage of the gross."

Nikki stopped squirming and stared up at him. "That's obscene."

"Indeed, it is," he agreed cheerfully, and bent his head to kiss her again.

Nikki turned her head sharply.

Pierce sighed against her temple. "You're not going to keep on pretending you don't want to kiss me as much as I want to kiss you, are you?" he whispered, nuzzling her ear as he spoke.

"Some of us don't feel it's necessary to get everything we want, whenever we happen to want it," she said stiffly, trying very hard not to be affected by the tenderness of the caress—or the feel of his hard, muscular body all along the length of hers.

"See?" he crowed at her inadvertent admission. "I was right. You *do* want to kiss me."

"I do not!"

He drew his head back to look down at her. "Prove it," he challenged.

Nikki just looked at him.

"Prove it," he said again. "Lie still and let me kiss you, and if you don't feel irresistibly compelled to kiss me back in, oh, say—" he slanted a teasing glance at her "—twenty minutes, I'll let you up and never bother you again."

Nikki sputtered on surprised, unwilling laughter. "That's ridiculous."

"But you're tempted, aren't you?"

Nikki tried to look stern. "I am not," she said, trying to believe it. Trying to make him believe it. "Not in the least."

"Oh, yes, you are," he said cajolingly. Knowingly. "I can tell these things about a woman. You're dying to kiss me but you don't want to admit it. Come on, Nikki." He nuzzled her cheek, brushing soft baby kisses over her tender skin. "Just one kiss. One—" he touched his lips to the corner of her mouth, urging her to turn her head just a bit more "—tiny...little—" his lips hovered over hers, as if waiting for permission "—kiss," he groaned as she turned her mouth up to his.

The kiss was deep and hot and sweet and—

"Ahem!" said a voice from the doorway.

Nikki stiffened and jerked her mouth from his, her muscles tensing, poised to scramble to her feet at the first opportunity. Pierce merely tightened his arms, holding her still, and lifted his head.

"Yes, Mrs. Gilmore?" he asked as calmly as if having his housekeeper catch him rolling around on the floor with a woman he'd just met was a daily occurrence. "What is it?"

"The reporters from *People* magazine are here," she said.

A bulb flashed over her left shoulder, confirming her statement.

Pierce shifted his gaze to the man with the camera. "I'd appreciate it if you wouldn't do that again," he said in a voice Nikki had never heard him use before.

Without a word, the photographer lowered his camera.

"Thank you," Pierce said, icily polite, and levered himself to his feet. He held out his hand and helped Nikki to hers. One look at her flushed, furious face told him she most definitely wouldn't care to stay and be introduced to his guests. "Why don't you meet with Kathy while I'm busy here?" he said, bending his head to hers so that his words couldn't be overheard. "She can give you my schedule for the next couple of days, go over the routine around here, that sort of thing. This interview won't take very long, and then we'll see about getting you settled in." He looked up at his housekeeper with a smile. "Mrs. Gilmore will show you where Kathy's office is."

"That's all right," Nikki said quickly. "I remember the way." Then, with a quick embarrassed nod, she did what every smart soldier does when faced with overwhelming odds. She retreated to regroup.

She hurried past the housekeeper and out the door of the garden room, following her nose down a short hallway with a sharp right angle and into Kathy Frye's pleasant office with its view of the pool and cabana area.

Kathy Frye wasn't in it. The hold button on the telephone was blinking madly, though, and a large leather-bound appointment book lay open on the desk's polished surface with a gold Cross pen laid carelessly across the lined page as if she'd been called away in the middle of some task. Presumably she would be back any minute.

Nikki sighed, thankful for even a few minutes alone to gather herself together. Her pulse was still beating wildly against the tender skin at the base of her throat, hard, as if she'd run a mile with a fifty-pound pack on her back. Her breasts were still tight and aching. Her lips still tingled. And all from just one kiss. She crossed her arms over her waist and turned toward the open glass doors, willing the unfamiliar feelings to go away.

She stared blindly for a second or two, her thoughts focused inward, and then, gradually, her gaze was drawn by the motionless figure of the gardener at the narrow end of the pool. She was kneeling in one of the flower beds that separated the pool from the terrazzo tiles of the patio area in front of the garden room. Her face was in profile to Nikki, her left hand up to shade her eyes, her right hand clutched around the handle of a small trowel. Intrigued by the woman's utter stillness, Nikki uncrossed her arms and stepped closer to the long, multipaned doors, her gaze following the direction of the gardener's focused stare.

She could see Pierce easily from where she stood, seated on one of the red chintz sofas in the garden room next to the reporter from *People* magazine. He was turned toward her slightly, his head tilted in what Nikki already recognized as a characteristic indication of attentiveness as the reporter spoke to him. He shook his head when she finished, obviously laughing at whatever she had said. The woman laughed with him, reaching out to touch his arm, lingeringly, as she did so.

And the gardener knelt there in the flower bed, as still as a statue, silently watching.

Nikki wondered if the woman had also been witness to *her* little tête-à-tête with Pierce. It was a discomforting thought. Even more discomforting was the thought of who else might have witnessed her near surrender to the charms of her employer. Because of the way the house was built—in a modified U-shape with the pool roughly in the middle—all of the rooms at the back were more-or-less visible to all the other rooms.

"It's a good idea to keep your bedroom drapes closed at night," said a voice behind her.

Nikki jumped and turned around.

"Sorry," Kathy said. "I didn't mean to startle you." She smiled as she went around behind her desk. "Just let me finish with this call and then I'm all yours," she said, stabbing the hold button with the eraser end of a pencil as she picked up the receiver.

Nikki turned back toward the open door to give the secretary some privacy for her call, feeling, unaccountably, as if she were violating the privacy of the woman in the flower bed by watching her watch Pierce. She reached out and pulled the doors closed.

"Poor Janice has it really bad," Kathy said a moment later as she came up beside Nikki at the glass. The faint scent of her perfume came with her.

"Janice?"

Kathy nodded her head toward the gardener, who had finally gone back to digging in the flower bed. "She's been mooning over Pierce ever since she started working here." Her smile just a bit derisive, as if she felt sympathy for the woman but found her ridiculous, too. "She's almost worse than Lisbeth sometimes."

"What do you mean, worse than Lisbeth?"

"Oh, she doesn't *do* anything, any more than Lisbeth does, if that's what you're getting at. She just follows him around with her eyes. Stares at him when he's not looking, like some hormone-ridden little teenybopper." She laughed softly. "But, hey, who can blame her, huh?" Kathy said, giving Nikki a conspiratorial little woman-to-woman look out of the corner of her eye. "That damned charm of his affects most of us that way, at least at first."

"Damned charm?" Nikki said, instantly picking up on the woman's word choice.

"Damned. Roguish. Rascally. Take your pick," Kathy said with a careless shrug. "The tabloids call him all that, and worse." She turned back to her desk, then, suddenly all business. "Mrs. Gilmore said Pierce wanted me to fill you in on the routine around here." She flipped the leather-bound appointment book back a few pages. "You're going to be real busy keeping track of him."

An hour later, the last of the clotted cream and scones were gone, Pierce had told several amusing anecdotes about the making of *The Devil's Game* and dropped a couple of hints about his next project, and several pictures had been taken of the movie star at his leisure. Finally the reporter from *People* put down her empty teacup and asked the question she'd been dying to ask since she'd walked into the garden room.

"So, the woman you were, ah . . . entertaining when we arrived—who is she?"

Pierce smiled wickedly. "Just a friend," he said, knowing the reporter would draw the correct incorrect conclusion. "A very good friend."

4

NIKKI CROSSED her arms over her chest like a stubborn child and pressed back into the soft leather seat of the Lamborghini. "I'm not getting out," she said, as Pierce maneuvered the car into a parking space.

He glanced over at her, his eyebrow raised inquiringly.

"I mean it. I have absolutely no desire to go shopping."

"Well, I do," Pierce said, and set the parking break with a gesture of finality. Without another word, he pushed open the door and stepped out of the flashy low-slung red car onto the hallowed ground of some of the most expensive and profitable real estate in the world with every expectation that Nikki would follow him.

Which, with an exasperated sigh, she did. It was, after all, what she'd been hired to do. "Oh, all right. All right. Hold on a minute," she said irritably, pushing open her own door without waiting for him to come around and do it for her. "I'm coming."

She glanced up and down the street as she stepped onto the curb, automatically checking for any suspicious-looking characters while he locked the car up tight. There were lots of characters hurrying up and down the crowded sidewalk, but not one of them looked as if they were poised to launch an attack on her famous charge's gorgeous person. A few of them— more than a few, actually, and most of those female—

glanced covertly at the man beside her but no more than that. It would have, she suspected, been considered less than cool for these hipper-than-hip Southern Californians to take any notice of something so commonplace as a mere movie star on Rodeo Drive. Nikki wished *something* would happen, though, that even just one overeager fan—an uncool tourist, maybe—would run screaming toward him. It would be as good an excuse as any to call a halt to this proposed shopping spree of his.

"Okay?" Pierce said as he turned from the car. He gave her a sardonic look, one that said he knew what she'd been doing—and thinking, probably. "Can we go now?"

"We can go," she answered. "But I'm only coming along on this little jaunt to protect you," she warned him. "I'm not going to buy anything."

"Fine," Pierce retorted. "Nobody asked you to." He reached out to take her hand in his.

She drew back instinctively, without thinking, putting her hand behind her, out of temptation's way.

Pierce gave her a knowing, faintly amused look. "You're supposed to be my new girlfriend, remember?" he said, reaching around her to take her hand in his. The movement brought him very close and he leaned even closer, putting his lips to her ear. Nikki was sure it must look as if he were nibbling on her. "We're supposed to be hot for each other," he murmured huskily, giving in to the temptation to nuzzle the soft, silky black hair at her temple.

She took a step back, tilting her head away and scowling fiercely in an effort to deny she'd felt anything at all, silently warning him to behave himself. "All right," she said, steeling herself to endure the little sparks that sizzled up and down her spine every time he touched her. "I'll try to pretend you make me weak in the knees." *Which won't*, she thought, *involve much pretense at all.* "But take my other hand, will you?" She pulled her right hand out of his grasp, reluctantly offering him her left as she stepped around to his other side. "That one's my gun hand."

"Jeez." He stopped on the sidewalk to look at her. "Don't tell me you're wearing your gun under that jacket."

"Well, of course I am. How do you expect me to protect you without it?"

He snorted inelegantly. "The only thing I'm going to need protection from on Rodeo Drive is salesclerks on commission," he said, and pushed open the door to a very small, very exclusive boutique.

It was decorated in burnished silver and soft grayed blue with lots of subdued lighting so as not to detract from the hideously expensive merchandise. There were no racks of clothing like in a normal boutique or department store, just several long-waisted, long-legged, arrogant-looking mannequins, tastefully dressed and posed to display the latest au courant styles and make the shopper think that she, too, could look like a rich, well-dressed anorexic if she just bought the right outfit.

It was the kind of place that had always intimidated Nikki in a way that no barking staff sergeant or smart-mouthed enlisted man on a weekend spree ever could, making her feel hopelessly unhip, badly dressed and as awkward as Gulliver in Lilliput. The beautifully dressed, professionally coifed salesclerks—each one as dainty and elegant as a porcelain doll—added immeasurably to Nikki's discomfort level, putting her in a worse mood than she'd been in to start with.

One of them glanced up at their entrance, the expression on her exquisite, expertly made-up face as bored and distant as those of the mannequins. It changed dramatically when she saw who'd come in to the store.

"Mr. Kingston," she said, hurrying forward to greet him as if he were a cross between visiting royalty and a naked Chippendale dancer. "What a pleasure to see you." Her smile glistened, beaming goodwill and helpfulness. Her eyes glowed, reflecting the expectation of a fat commission. "What can I do for you today?"

"Hello, Marla," Pierce said warmly, effortlessly calling up the salesclerk's name from what Nikki was sure must be the vast store of feminine names warehoused in his libidinous synapses.

The young woman's face brightened even more at this sign of recognition, the gleam in her eyes becoming a little less monetary as obvious fantasies of romance—implied by the fact of his remembering her name—began to flicker through her mind.

"We'd like to look at some dresses," Pierce said, ignoring Nikki's inarticulate sound of protest. He squeezed her hand, preventing her from withdrawing it from his, and glanced down at her long, jeans-clad legs and then back up again, giving her a playfully lascivious wink. "Short dresses," he said, his voice and expression all business as he turned back to the salesclerk.

"Day or evening?" the young woman inquired in an equally businesslike tone as her fleeting fantasies of romance faded under the reality of Pierce Kingston's obvious fascination with the exotic dark-haired woman by his side. A fat commission check would have to suffice.

"Evening," Pierce said, with another quick glance at Nikki. In her black leather bomber jacket and cowboy boots, with a white T-shirt tucked into a pair of skintight jeans, her daytime look was right in step with current Tinsel Town fashion trends.

"Any preference as to color or style?"

"Nikki?" Pierce said.

She glared at him, stubbornly refusing to answer.

He grinned. "Simple styles," he said to the salesclerk. "Sleek and narrow and not too fussy. Maybe one of those skinny little dresses that look like a slip. And one of those slinky numbers made with lots of spandex." He glanced at Nikki's set face, then let his gaze drift down her body. "Yeah, definitely one of those spandex dresses," he said, thoroughly enjoying himself. "And a leather miniskirt like the one on that mannequin over there." He lifted a suggestive eyebrow. "I have a real thing for ladies in leather," he said, his voice low and confiding. He brushed the fingers of his free hand down the arm of Nikki's black leather bomber jacket to emphasize the point. "In a size—" he cast another assessing, caressing glance down Nikki's long, lean body, from the top of her feathery haircut to the toes of her cowboy boots, "—eight?" he guessed.

Nikki stared straight ahead, refusing to answer him. He *would* be able to tell her size just by looking, she fumed silently. He'd undoubtedly had lots and lots of experience in buying clothes for women. And in this store, too, if the avaricious gleam in the salesclerk's eyes was anything to go by. Well, he wasn't buying any clothes for her!

"Colors?" the salesclerk asked.

"Vivid," Pierce said with authority. "Red, black, bright purple, hot pink. Green, if you've got it in a shade to match her eyes. And something with a little flash and sparkle, too. Maybe with sequins, if you have it. We're going to a premiere in a couple of weeks," he explained, glancing at Nikki for her reaction to that bit of information.

She continued to ignore him. The clerk smiled and nodded and went away to find what he'd asked for.

"You're wasting your time," Nikki hissed when the young woman was out of earshot. "I'm not going to wear anything she brings out here. I'm not even going to try it on."

"It's my time to waste," Pierce said pleasantly. "And you are, too, going to try it on. Because I'm going to insist."

"You can insist until doomsday but it isn't going to do you any good. I'm not going to wear any of these overpriced glad rags."

"We discussed this last night after you brought your stuff to the house, didn't we? And again this morning at breakfast," he said, still more amused than impatient with her intractability. "I thought you understood that as my live-in lover you're going to need a larger, more extravagant wardrobe than you have at present."

"And I thought *you* understood that I can't afford a more extravagant wardrobe. Especially one that comes from Rodeo Drive."

"Which is why I'm paying for it."

"No," Nikki said. "You're not. And neither am—"

"Here we are." The salesclerk swooped back into the showroom with at least a dozen dresses on a rolling clothes rack. "These are just my first selections. I have others if none of these are what you had in mind."

"These will do just fine to start with," Pierce assured her. He turned his gaze on Nikki. "Won't they, darling?"

"No, they won't," Nikki snapped back at him under her breath.

Pierce smiled at the salesclerk. "Why don't you take those to a dressing room, Marla?" he suggested graciously, as unconcerned as if stubborn women who turned down expensive new clothes were an everyday occurrence when, in his experience, just the opposite was true. Woman never turned down gifts from him. Especially not expensive gifts. "We'll be there in a moment."

He waited until the salesclerk had retreated. "Look," he said turning back to Nikki with the exaggerated patience of an adult dealing with a fractious, unreasonable child, "just what exactly is your problem with this?"

"My problem," Nikki said, looking at him in a way that was anything but childlike, "is that I'm not some little tootsie who lets men she hardly knows buy her expensive gifts."

"It isn't a gift. Not the way you mean it, anyway." He smiled cajolingly. "If it'll make you feel better, think of it as one of the perks of the job."

"I don't want any special perks, either," she said huffily, affronted by the suggestion that mere semantics would make a difference to her.

"Think of it as a requirement, then," he snapped, his amusement finally giving way to impatience.

Nikki narrowed her eyes and glared at him.

Pierce narrowed his eyes and glared back at her.

A full five seconds passed as they stood there, hands clasped, and tried to frown each other into submission.

"I'll make a scene," Pierce warned.

"You wouldn't."

"Yes, I would," he said with relish. "A huge, noisy scene that'll turn that pretty face of yours bright red with embarrassment." He tapped her nose with his forefinger to emphasize the point and grinned his pirate's grin. "And I think you already know that it wouldn't embarrass me in the least."

Nikki knew. Even on the basis of barely two day's acquaintance, she knew. The man had absolutely no sense of decorum or self-consciousness; too many people had been staring at him for too long for it to bother him. *I shouldn't let it bother me, either*, she told herself. *I'm made of sterner stuff than that.* And if they were someplace else—on a military base or in the middle of a war zone, say, or anyplace where she was indisputably in charge—it *wouldn't* bother her. But in the middle of Beverly Hills, in a ritzy store with snooty salesclerks, with a man she couldn't threaten to throw into the brig if he didn't behave himself . . . and never mind the unnerving fact that her knees tended to disintegrate to the consistency of overcooked noodles every time he smiled at her.

"You're a snake," she said, in a quiet voice. "An unprincipled, low-down, no-good, conniving, manipulating snake."

Pierce's grin widened. "Does that mean we'll do this my way?"

"Yes, damn it," she hissed, giving in with absolutely no attempt at accepting defeat gracefully. "I'll try them on. But once we're out of here I won't wear them anywhere. Ever."

"STUPID SHOES," Nikki muttered, frowning down at the black spike heels Pierce Kingston had picked out to go with the "slinky black number" she was wearing. If she hadn't been quick enough to catch herself on the newel post, she'd be sprawled face down on the kitchen floor. As it was, she'd dropped her purse when she reached out to break her fall, sending the contents flying in all directions across the tile.

Lisbeth Greene, sitting at the kitchen table in the same chair she'd occupied yesterday afternoon, glanced up from under her wispy bangs, sniffed and went back to taking notes from the open textbook in front of her.

With a muffled oath, Nikki crouched down and began gathering her scattered possessions. "I'm fine," she said, as if Lisbeth had expressed concern. "No damage done."

Lisbeth still didn't move from her chair at the table. "Do you need any help?" she asked finally, surreptitiously watching Nikki's head bob up and down as she scooted around in search of loose change, old receipts and stray ballpoint pens.

"That's really sweet of you, Lisbeth, but I think I've got everything. Except . . ." Her voice trailed off. "Ah, there it is," she said, reaching under the table. Her arm wasn't quite long enough. "Could you reach down and get that for me, please, Lisbeth? It's right by your foot."

"Get what?" Lisbeth asked in a bored voice. But she bent down to look. Her eyes rounded in surprise as they met Nikki's under the table. "Is that a *real* gun?" she asked, suddenly sounding much younger than the nineteen years Nikki knew her to be.

"A 9mm Baretta," Nikki said as she backed out from under the table and got to her feet. "So pick it up carefully. By the butt, please."

Lisbeth reached down and picked up the pistol in two fingers. "Do you always carry a gun?" she asked, holding it out toward Nikki.

"When I'm working, yes," Nikki said. "Always."

"Are you a good shot?" Lisbeth asked, watching as Nikki checked the pistol for damage.

"It wouldn't make much sense to carry it if I wasn't, now would it?" Nikki said, making sure the safety was in place before putting the gun back into her purse.

"Wow. I guess you really are a bodyguard."

Nikki lifted an eyebrow. "Did you think I wasn't?"

Lisbeth shrugged and looked away, obviously uncomfortable with the question. "I dunno," she mumbled.

"Well, I can assure you, I am—"

"Ah, Miss Martinelli, there you are," Marjorie Gilmore said as she came into the kitchen with a cut-crystal vase in each hand. "Mr. Kingston was just wondering if you were ready yet."

Nikki grimaced. "As ready as I'll ever be, I guess," she said, and tugged at the hem of her dress.

"You look very nice," Lisbeth said, offering a small, guarded smile. "Doesn't she look nice, Aunt Margie?" she added, looking to her aunt for confirmation.

Marjorie Gilmore glanced up from the sink where she was preparing to wash the vases. "Very nice," she said, her clipped tones making Nikki feel like an underdressed bimbo.

Or more of a bimbo, anyway, than she had standing in front of the mirror in her room upstairs. She tugged at the hem of the stretchy black dress again, wishing it came a little farther down on her thighs and wondering what was going to happen when she sat in it. Four years in a marine uniform didn't prepare a woman for the rigors of wearing civilian evening clothes, especially a woman who'd grown up as a dress-hating tomboy who'd always preferred to wear exactly what her four older brothers wore because it made her feel more like one of the boys.

But one couldn't really get away with wearing old jeans or motorcycle leathers to a taping of the "Arsenio Hall" show. Unless the jeans were custom shredded by Calvin Klein. And the leathers were jewel-studded Chanel originals. And you were either as outrageous as Cher or as famous as Elizabeth Taylor. Or both.

Not that Nikki was actually going to be *on* "Arsenio Hall." She had absolutely put her foot down on that. But she would be backstage while Pierce went on. And then—*Oh, joy!* she thought with dread—they were going out to dinner afterward. And even she had to admit that her conservative red suit with the slim knee-length skirt and boxy jacket wouldn't cut it on the Hollywood glamour circuit; she didn't have to be hit over the head with a lead pipe to realize that Pierce Kingston and his ilk didn't date women who dressed like somebody's secretary.

So here she was, decked out in a dress that was too short and earrings that were too long and high heels that made her wonder if she was risking a broken ankle for the sake of a job.

"I feel like ten pounds of pork stuffed into a five-pound-sausage casing in this thing," Nikki said.

"Oh, no," Lisbeth assured her, with another small smile. "You look just like a model. You could be Robin Givens's partner on 'Angel Street.'"

"Thanks," Nikki said, surprised that Lisbeth had unbent enough to actually compliment her.

Ten minutes ago, Nikki would have sworn the young woman would have cheered if she'd broken her neck falling down the stairs. Now here she was, acting almost friendly. *Because she believes I'm a real bodyguard now and not competition for the lord of the manor?* Nikki mused, wondering if the whole fan letter thing could be solved as easily as that.

"Was there something you wanted in the kitchen, Miss Martinelli?" the housekeeper asked pointedly when Nikki continued to stand there, staring thoughtfully at her niece.

"Wanted? Oh, yes. Pepto," Nikki remembered. "I came down here to see if you had any Pepto-Bismol. I couldn't find any in the guest bathroom."

"We don't keep it in the kitchen," Mrs. Gilmore said, as if Nikki should have known that. "But I'm sure there's some in the supply closet upstairs. Lisbeth will get it for you."

"No. No, that's all right." Nikki waved Lisbeth back down in her chair, trying to sneak a peek at the girl's notebook without being obvious about it. "I don't want to interrupt your studying," she said, realizing she couldn't tell anything about the handwriting by trying to read it upside down. She gave up the effort and pulled open the double-wide stainless steel door of the refrigerator. "I'll just have some milk instead. That'll settle my stomach just as well as the Pepto."

"Don't you feel good?" Lisbeth asked.

"It's just nerves." Nikki reached for a carton of milk. "I've never been out to dinner with a movie star before."

"Get Miss Martinelli a glass, Lisbeth," Marjorie Gilmore said, as if she thought Nikki were going to drink straight from the carton.

For a second, Nikki contemplated doing exactly that, just to see the expression on the housekeeper's face. But her innate good manners and her mother's training asserted themselves, and she took the glass that Lisbeth held out to her. "Thanks," she said, smiling at the younger woman.

Lisbeth smiled back for the third time in as many minutes. Although it wasn't exactly part of her job description—she'd only been hired to protect Pierce, not find out who'd been writing him mash notes—Nikki decided to do a little probing. "You wouldn't want to go tonight in my place, would you?" she asked as she poured milk into her glass.

"Don't you want to go?"

Nikki shrugged. "Not particularly," she said, and chugged back half a glass of milk in three long gulps. She felt her earrings brush against her bare collarbone with the movement.

"Not even with Pierce?" Lisbeth persisted, as if the thought of any female being so wrongheaded was completely inconceivable to her.

"Not particularly," Nikki said again, casually, as though it were the exact, unvarnished truth. "Pierce is just another job to me," she said. "I have absolutely no interest in him as a man."

"You don't?"

"He's not my type at all." The lie slipped out easily, considering its gargantuan proportions; Nikki wondered why she didn't choke on it. "As far as I'm concerned, he's fair game for any woman who wants him. Except, of course," she added, watching Lisbeth for a reaction, "for whoever's writing those creepy fan letters."

"Hey, anybody there seen my bodyguard?" Pierce's disembodied voice floated down the back stairs.

And Nikki lost Lisbeth's attention between one breath and the next.

"I went up to her room to see what was keeping her and—ah, there you are," he said, his blue eyes zeroing in on Nikki as he came into the kitchen. He smiled with a very masculine sort of pleasure, satisfaction radiating through him at the sight of her standing in front of the refrigerator in the little black dress he'd bought for her. He didn't pause to wonder why the sight of her, wearing a dress he'd provided, pleased him so much. He only knew that it did. "I knew that dress would suit you," he said.

He didn't seem to notice Lisbeth sitting there, staring at him with a look of worshipful adoration on her face, but Nikki did. And so, if she wasn't mistaken, did Lisbeth's aunt. And Lisbeth's aunt didn't like it one little bit. Nikki wondered why.

Was it simple distaste for her niece's very obvious infatuation that irked the uptight housekeeper? Was it Pierce's seeming insensitivity to her niece's feelings? Or was it something more sinister? Something like . . . jealousy, perhaps? Nikki pondered the possibility for a moment, clearly recalling the disapproving, tight-lipped expression the housekeeper had had on her face when she'd caught her employer and his new bodyguard rolling around on the floor of the garden room yesterday.

But Marjorie Gilmore is old enough to be Pierce's grandmother, Nikki reminded herself, scowling at the glass in her hand as she tried to sort things out in her mind. *Or his mother, at least. And, anyway, she's been with him for years. Hasn't she?* It was ridiculous to think she'd suddenly taken to writing weird love letters to her boss. Wasn't it?

"Short skirts were definitely the way to go," Pierce said, smiling wolfishly when Nikki looked up at him. "You look terrific," he told her, ogling her legs. He made a twirling motion with his hand. "Turn around so I can see the back," he ordered, anticipating the sight of the stretchy black fabric molded to her heart-shaped little bottom.

Nikki steeled herself against the warm fuzzy feelings his compliments caused and gave him a look that would freeze lava.

Pierce grinned. "No?" he said, unaffected by her refusal to cooperate. "Well, finish your milk then, so we can go. We don't want to keep Arsenio waiting."

5

I KNEW THIS WOULD HAPPEN when I sat down, Nikki thought, surreptitiously tugging at the hem of her dress as she tried to find the best position for her legs in the small amount of space available in the passenger seat of the Lamborghini. It had been a feat of grace and dexterity just getting into the car without exposing her all. She didn't even want to *think* about how she was going to hoist herself out of the low-slung automobile without sacrificing what was left of her modesty to the night air and Pierce Kingston's avid eyes. She pressed her knees together, angling them to give herself more room, and refused to worry about it until she had to.

"I thought that Lisbeth didn't live here with you and her aunt," she said, to give herself something else to think about.

"She doesn't." Pierce downshifted, slowing the car to check for traffic as they came through the open iron gates at the end of the driveway, then shifted again as he accelerated onto the street. The engine gave a satisfying rumble of power. "She lives in a dorm room at U.C.L.A."

"Really? She seems to spend an awful lot of time in your kitchen."

Pierce slanted a glance at her. "So?"

"So, you'd think a girl that age would want to hang out with her friends."

"You'd think," Pierce agreed absently.

"Do you know why she doesn't?"

"Doesn't what?" Pierce said, more interested in the way Nikki's skirt was inching up her thighs again than in what she was saying. *Luscious thighs,* he thought, silently giving thanks for spandex and memory yarn.

"Doesn't hang out with her friends," Nikki persisted.

"Whose friends?" *World-class thighs,* he thought. They were smooth and firm, with a hint of definition running down the sides between the front and back quadriceps muscles. *Strong thighs.* He felt his blood heat a few degrees more as both he and the car shifted into second.

"Lisbeth's friends," Nikki said in exasperation. "Pierce—" she angled herself a bit more in the seat "—are you listening to me?"

Pierce's hands tightened on the steering wheel as the hem of her dress rose another inch higher on her thighs. "Every word," he said, although he would have been hard-pressed to repeat those words back to her.

"Well, don't you think it's odd that she spends so much time with her aunt?"

"Who?"

"Lisbeth!" she said, the annoyance clear in her voice. She turned to face him more fully, completely forgetting about the hem of her dress. "Don't you think—" She broke off as she caught the direction of his gaze. "Oh, for heaven's sake." She shifted in her seat, pointing her knees toward the dashboard and yanking her dress down as far as it would go. "Don't you ever think of anything else?" she asked, holding the material in place with the flat of her hands.

"Not when I'm around you, it seems."

It took Nikki a second or two to fight down the spurt of pleasure his words gave her, but she did it. "Does that line actually work?" she asked, managing to inject a credible amount of acrimony into her voice.

"It isn't a line."

"Yeah, right." She made a small sound of disgust. "And I'm the tooth fairy."

"I don't use lines," Pierce said, unaccountably stung by her disbelief. He'd been completely sincere in all his dealings with her. "I don't ha—" He broke off, as if suddenly realizing how conceited it would sound.

"Because you don't have to," Nikki finished for him, her tone as tart as straight lemon juice.

Pierce couldn't help but smile at her acerbity. "All right, yes," he said, because it was true—and because he wanted to hear what she'd have to say to that. "I don't have to."

"Women just fall into your lap like ripe plums, is that it?" she said, thinking of Lisbeth and Janice and the salesclerk at the boutique. And herself, if she was crazy enough to let it happen.

"That's it," Pierce agreed. He waited a beat. "You feeling ripe yet?"

She shot him a killing glance out of the corner of her eye. "I'll rot on the vine before I stand in line for some man again."

"Again?" he asked, picking up on the one word she wished she hadn't uttered.

"It's none of your business," she said flatly, in a tone that brooked no argument.

Pierce backed off immediately, sensing the bitterness and hurt beneath her words. Here was an interesting bit of information, he thought. A love affair gone bad. *I'll rot on the vine before I stand in line for some man again.* That meant whoever it was had cheated on her. The idiot. Pierce couldn't understand that kind of behavior. He'd been with a lot of women in his life—not nearly as many as he'd been credited with, but a lot. And there had never been more than one woman at a time. They'd sometimes followed pretty closely on each other's heels—especially in his younger, wilder years—but they'd never overlapped.

Simply by watching his father he'd learned, first-hand, what kind of destruction and pain lay down that path and he'd vowed, years ago, never to travel it himself. Despite his colorful reputation as a love-'em-and-leave-'em playboy, it was a vow he took very seriously. Yesterday, after the reporter from *People* left, he'd called Alanna Fairchild to say his goodbyes. The ending was a little more abrupt than he would have liked—in the timing, if nothing else—but he and Alanna had both known the relationship would never be more than physical and she professed to have no hard feelings.

It wouldn't have made any difference if she had, he realized a little uneasily, glancing over at the silent woman beside him. He'd set his sights on Nikki Martinelli the minute she walked into his garden room in her high-heeled cowboy boots and tight leather pants. It wasn't just her body—although, Lord knows, he thought, glancing at her again, she made his mouth water with anticipation. It was something else. Something *more.* Something in the tilt of her chin and the gleam in her remarkable green eyes. Something in the way she planted her feet and stood her ground, challenging him, even though any fool could see he scared her spitless, way down deep at some basic man-woman level.

Which was another thing that intrigued him. All his life, women had desired him, fawned over him, flattered him and flirted with him. They threw themselves at his head or, as she had so aptly stated, fell into his lap like ripe plums, but none in his memory had ever been afraid of him.

He wondered if that hint of vulnerability, that fawnlike wariness, peeking out from beneath her tough cookie facade was another thing that could be laid at the door of the man who'd taught her the futility of waiting in line.

He reached over and touched her hand lightly. "I'm sorry," he said softly, meaning it.

She turned her head slowly and looked at him, obviously surprised by his admission. "For what?" she asked suspiciously.

"You were trying to talk to me like a rational human being," he said, "and I was acting like a jackass."

"Yes," Nikki said, a trace of asperity still in her voice. "You were."

"Do you forgive me?"

I shouldn't, Nikki thought. *If I knew what was good for me, I wouldn't.* "Are you ready to talk seriously?" she asked.

He nodded.

"Without jokes?" she insisted. "Or . . . or leering innuendo?"

"On my honor as a Kingston," he said solemnly, vowing to keep his eyes strictly on the road and off her legs. At least for now.

"TELL US ABOUT *The Devil's Game*," Arsenio Hall suggested, leaning forward in his chair as if he were encouraging the telling of scandalous secrets. "The buzz around town says it's going to be *the* blockbuster movie of the summer."

Sitting in front of the monitor in the greenroom—which wasn't green at all—Nikki watched Pierce flash a modest grin and proceed to tell Arsenio and his audience just what made his new action-adventure epic different from every other action-adventure movie ever made. She was amazed at how relaxed and natural he appeared under the merciless scrutiny of the lights and cameras, how easily he made blatant promotional plugs sound like normal conversation.

Sitting on set with the late-night talk-show host, he exuded warmth and charm and an effortless, straightforward, unapologetic sex appeal that had the women in the audience squirming in their seats, and the men thinking he was the kind of guy they wouldn't mind sharing a few beers with. Nikki smiled to herself, wondering what those men would think if they knew the man on the stage was wearing nearly as much makeup as the female jazz singer who'd preceded him. *That* would blow his superstud image all to hell.

And then again, maybe it wouldn't.

She, after all, had stood guard by his swivel chair while the show's makeup artist had applied foundation and mascara and—because "the lights wash all the color out of your face"—even a faint dusting of blusher, and it hadn't affected *her* opinion of his masculinity one iota. If anything, it had reenforced it. Any man who could look macho while wearing mascara was too rampantly male for anything short of a sex-change operation to threaten his virility.

"Are we ready for the clip now?" Arsenio asked someone off camera when Pierce had finished setting up the bare bones of the preview scene for the audience.

Apparently they were, because the image on the monitor suddenly switched from the stage in the Burbank studio to the steamy interior of some unspecified Central American country. Dressed in faded fatigues, with an automatic Mauser tucked into his waistband, a twelve-inch hunting knife strapped to his thigh, and an all-too-realistic gash on his temple slowly oozing blood down the side of his face, Pierce appeared to be slogging his way through a guerrilla-infested jungle with an Uzi slung over one shoulder and an unconscious woman over the other. She began to struggle weakly.

"Hold still, goddamn it," he hissed, clamping his arm tighter over her thrashing legs.

She continued to struggle until he stopped and let her slide down his body. Her face filled the screen as she looked up at him. Her eyes went wide.

"Luc," she breathed.

"Did you think I wouldn't find you?" he demanded fiercely, fisting a hand in her long dark hair as he pulled her head back. "Did you really think I'd let you get away?"

"Luc, I…" Her fingers curled in the fabric of his dirty fatigue shirt. "Please," she said.

Their lips met in a searing, openmouthed kiss.

In the studio audience, women squealed and hooted, hollering for more. In the green room, Nikki curled her fingers against the urge to yank every strand of hair from the actress's head. On the screen, the scene faded briefly to black and then faded back in on the face of the host. He grinned and fanned himself. "I'd *heard* you and your leading lady were hot together." His smile turned coaxing, inviting confidences. "Is it true you were just as hot off the screen?"

"Andie MacDowell is a happily married woman," Pierce said easily, showing absolutely no sign that he hated those kinds of personal questions. "And I'm involved with someone else. Someone," he added with a grin, "who wouldn't like it if I talked about our relationship on national television."

Nikki, along with every other woman in the viewing audience, wondered just who the lucky woman was while Arsenio Hall thanked his guest for appearing on the show.

PIERCE HANDED his keys to the parking valet and took Nikki's hand in his. "I thought we'd start out slow," he said, explaining his choice of Chasen's over the more trendy Mortons or Spago for dinner. "We need to get used to being seen in public together. And we need to agree to some ground rules before we go inside," he added, as they headed toward the entrance to one of the favorite restaurants of Hollywood's old guard.

"Ground rules?" Nikki said skeptically. "What kind of ground rules? Why?"

"So you don't try to give me a karate chop to the neck if I put my arm around you."

Nikki shot him a sidelong look. "I didn't realize you were planning to put your arm around me."

"I'm not planning it," he said, although that was exactly what he was planning. That and anything else she'd let him get away with. "But it might happen naturally in the course of the evening."

She gave him a wry look. "During dinner?"

He sighed. Deeply. "We're supposed to be fostering the impression that we're having the hottest romance of the decade," he said in an aggrieved voice. "Under those circumstances I don't think an occasional hug is out of line." He glanced at her out of the corner of his eye in an effort to gauge her reaction to his next words. "You might even try hugging me back."

"What about the woman you're involved with? How is she going to feel about all this public fondling of a woman who isn't her?"

Pierce came to a stop in front of the door to the restaurant, pulling Nikki to a halt beside him. "What woman are you talking about?"

"The one who wouldn't like it if you talked about your relationship on national television. I hardly think she'd like it any better if it got back to her that you were snuggling up to some woman in a fancy restaurant."

Pierce grinned, pleased by her reaction to the thought of another woman. "Oh, *that* woman."

Nikki arched a brow. "Yes, *that* woman."

Pierce shrugged. "She's nobody for you to worry about."

"Nobody for me to—" she began indignantly.

"She's a figment of my imagination," Pierce said. And it was almost true. The relationship he wanted with Nikki was still only a figment of his imagination. "A convenient ruse to stop people from asking questions that are none of their business."

Nikki considered that for a moment. "Oh. Okay," she decided, trying not to reveal the sense of euphoria that suddenly swamped her. *The other woman isn't real!* "I'll buy that," she said with a casual attempt at a shrug.

"So we're agreed then?"

"On what?"

"The ground rules. We'll hold hands. I'll hug you once or twice. I might even throw in a kiss if it seems warranted. A little kiss," he added quickly, before she could object. "Like this." He lifted their clasped hands to his mouth and kissed the back of her wrist. "See? No big deal."

"No big deal," Nikki echoed, trying to make her wildly beating heart believe it as they stood there in front of Chasens, staring at each other as if they were the only two people in the world.

"Excuse me," said a deep masculine voice.

Pierce looked up. "Mr. Peck," he said respectfully, stepping out of the other man's way. "How are you, sir?"

"Very well, thank you, Pierce," the legendary actor said with a dignified nod. There was an amused glint in his eyes. "Carry on," he said as he stepped around them and continued into the restaurant.

Nikki clutched at Pierce's hand. "That was Gregory Peck," she said in an excited little voice. "You said hello to Gregory Peck. He knew your name."

"He's an old friend of my parents. I've known him since I was a little kid."

"I saw him and your mother in *Vow of Silence* when I was fifteen," Nikki said in a hushed voice. "I thought it was the saddest, most romantic movie I'd ever seen. I still do." She sighed. "Gregory Peck. I can't believe it. Gregory Peck knows who you are." She gave Pierce a teasing grin. "I'm really impressed."

"If you like, I'll introduce you," Pierce said, as if he were offering her a bribe. "Later. After I see how well you follow the ground rules."

6

PIERCE KINGSTON'S hot new romance was hot news the
very next morning.

The *Star* had somehow gotten hold of the picture that
had been taken in the garden room by the photographer from *People* and enlarged it to cover most of the
front page. It showed Pierce's face clearly, but Nikki,
lying under him with her head buried in his shoulder,
was identified only as "an exotic, dark-haired mystery
woman" who had moved in with him after a whirl-
wind romance. Much was made of the fact that "legendary ladies' man, Pierce Kingston," had never had a
live-in lover, and wedding bells, it was hinted, had already rung over the pair in a hush-and-hurry Las Vegas ceremony.

The *National Enquirer* had to make do with less tit-
illating photographs snapped the previous evening as
Pierce and Nikki were coming out of Chasen's but they
had her name—and a grainy snapshot of her in her
MP's uniform. The headline, at least an inch high, read
The Star And The Soldier. After giving the highlights
of her four-year career in the marines and lauding her
"heroic contributions to the American effort in the recent Gulf War," it went on to give the purported details
of her current romance with Hollywood's sexiest leading man. The tabloid had decided she was a stunt-
woman—an occupation she had tried when she first
moved to Los Angeles and quickly given up as too

dangerous—apparently because it could then report that she and Pierce had met while working on the set of *The Devil's Game*. According to the paper's sources, the two of them had "looked into each other's eyes and fallen instantly in love." Since Pierce had never before had a live-in lover, they too were hinting at the possibility of wedding bells.

Talk-show hostess Joan Rivers opened the gossip segment of her morning program with the story.

USA Today devoted a paragraph to it in their "Lifestyle" section.

And "CNN Headline News" gave it a mention in their "Hollywood Minute" segment.

Pierce grinned with satisfaction when Kathy Frye informed him he'd warranted CNN coverage. "Did Dennis Michael actually mention *The Devil's Game?*" he asked her.

Kathy's smile mirrored his. "Twice."

"Good." He took a sip of his black coffee. "Good. Make sure Claire knows, will you?" he said, looking at his secretary over the rims of his reading glasses. "She likes to keep track of that sort of thing."

"Good?" Nikki said from across the table. "They print this trash about us, and you call it good? It's full of innuendo and downright lies."

"Yes, but they mentioned the movie," Kathy said. "That's the important thing." She handed Pierce his morning mail with the current copy of *People* magazine displayed prominently on top of the stack. Pierce's own face stared back at him from the cover, his lips turned up in what Nikki thought of as his pirate's grin. "It's a good article," Kathy said. "They concentrated mostly on the movie. Used the stills I gave them of you and Ms. MacDowell on the set of *The Devil's Game.*

And an old picture of you with your whole family at Gage and Tara's wedding. They only mention the mystery woman—" she glanced at Nikki "—twice, in passing."

Pierce nodded. "Anything else that requires my urgent attention today?"

Kathy looked down at her notebook. "*Esquire* called. They want to discuss a possible cover article. Claire wants you to call her this afternoon around four. She says a decision has to be made about a director for the new script. You need to make a decision on those three invitations—" she nodded at the small stack of mail "—as soon as possible so I can RSVP one way or the other. And there's a pile of letters on my desk that are waiting for your review and signature sometime today. There's also that batch of new publicity photos you've been putting off autographing. We're going to need them soon," she told him. "The old supply is running low."

Pierce sighed, thinking of the writer's cramp he was going to suffer. "I'll do a bunch of them right after breakfast, okay?"

"I could sign them and save us both a lot of time and trouble," Kathy offered. "No one will know the difference."

Pierce shook his head. "I'll know," he said. He received so much fan mail that it was impossible for him to answer each one individually—although he did try to read them all—but he firmly believed that anyone who took the time to write to him deserved a picture autographed in his own hand in return, at least.

Kathy nodded and flipped her notebook closed. She took a deep breath. "There's one more thing," she said.

Pierce raised an eyebrow at her tone.

"It might be nothing," she hedged, obviously uncomfortable with what she was about to say. "I might be seeing problems where there aren't any but, well— here." She put a crumpled sheet of lined, pastel blue notepaper down on the table. "It's a note from Lisbeth to her aunt."

Pierce looked up at his secretary. "So why are you giving it to me?"

"Pierce, don't be dense," Nikki said. "She's giving it to you because it's the same kind of paper those fan letters were written on."

"You think *Lisbeth* is writing those letters?" He looked back and forth between the two women as if he couldn't believe what he was hearing. "Lisbeth is just a kid. A shy kid, at that."

"Lisbeth is a young woman," Nikki said. "And shy or not, she's got a humongous crush on you. She's around all the time—"

"Visiting her aunt! This is her first year away from home and Mrs. Gilmore is the only family she has out here. The kid hangs around here because she's homesick."

"Maybe," Nikki said. "And maybe she hangs around to be near you."

"Those letters come through the mail," Pierce pointed out. He gestured at the crumpled note on the table between them. "They aren't left lying around the house for anyone to find."

"It wasn't lying around," Kathy said. "I found it on the floor next to the trash can in the kitchen."

"And that's exactly where it should go," Pierce said. "In the trash."

"You should at least compare the handwriting," Nikki said quietly.

"You compare it," Pierce replied, glancing at the note with an expression of distaste. "I never believed that whoever wrote those letters posed any real threat to begin with. And even if I did believe it, I sure as hell wouldn't believe it was Lisbeth Greene. That's ridiculous. In the first place, she hasn't got it in her to write stuff like that. In the second place, you can buy that kind of notepaper in any stationery or office supply store in the country. And in the third place..." He gave a snort of disgust. "Hell, I might just as well suspect Mrs. Gilmore or—" he flung a hand toward his secretary "—or Kathy. Or you."

"Nobody's saying it's Lisbeth. Or anyone else, at this point." Nikki reached out to pick up the note as she spoke. "But burying your head in the sand won't prove it one way or another."

"Why don't you have it dusted for fingerprints while you're at it?"

Nikki gave him a reproachful glare. "Your attitude isn't helping any," she said, and lowered her gaze to read the note.

The handwriting was rounded and flowing, the letters full of loops and swirls, a bit childish, a bit fanciful. It resembled the handwriting in the fan letters, but was it the same handwriting? Without one of the letters to compare it to, Nikki couldn't tell. Maybe even with the letters to compare it to, she wouldn't be able to tell.

"I'm no handwriting expert," she said at last.

Pierce snorted derisively.

"I think we should have someone who is take a look at this. If Claire doesn't know anyone who can do it," Nikki said as she handed the note to Kathy, "I can give her the names of a couple of people who can."

Kathy took the pale blue sheet of paper and turned to go.

"Kathy?" Pierce said, halting her.

She turned her head inquiringly. "I'll need reservations tonight at Spago," he said. "Dinner for two at eight o'clock." He looked across the table at Nikki. "If you're right and there is some crazy fan out there, then it's time we did something to bring her out of the woodwork and into the open. If I'm right, then we'll put this foolishness to rest, once and for all."

"I DON'T THINK this is a good idea," Nikki said, eyeing the fans and photographers loitering around the entrance to the restaurant from the inside of Pierce's Rolls-Royce limousine. "Crowds make it difficult for me to do my job effectively."

"Relax," Pierce advised her, leaning back against the seat as he waited for the driver to come around and open the door. "They're not waiting around to see us, specifically. They're just hoping to see a movie star. Any movie star."

Nikki hitched the long strap of her purse up on her shoulder, hefting the reassuring weight of her gun, and put a hand on the hem of her red leather miniskirt to keep it from riding up on her thighs. "I still think you should reconsider," she said, carefully scooting toward the door in order to get out first. She already knew he wasn't going to take her advice, and she wanted to put herself between him and possible danger.

"You and Claire think I have a dangerous fan out there—" he waved a hand "—somewhere, close at hand, waiting to do me bodily harm for being unfaithful. If that's true, then the best way to flush her out is to wave my infidelity—which is you—" he touched her

nose with his fingertip"—in front of her like a red flag.
So the more publicity she reads about the two of us, the
better. Smile for the photographers, darling," he said
as the driver pulled the car door open with a flourish.
Somehow, despite her careful maneuvering, Pierce
managed to step out of the long black limousine first.

"Oh, look, it's Pierce Kingston," someone squealed.

"I loved you in *The Promise*," someone else hollered
as he reached back into the car to offer Nikki a hand.

"Could I have your autograph, Mr. Kingston?" A
small pink imitation leather book with a pen attached
on a satin ribbon was thrust practically under his nose.

Pierce let go of Nikki's hand to take it.

"Sign it to Millie," the woman said, staring up at him
with adoring eyes.

"Are the rumors true?" demanded a photographer as
Pierce obligingly signed half-a-dozen other autographs. "Was there a secret ceremony in Las Vegas? Are
you and Nikki married?"

"Not yet," Pierce said. With a warm smile, he handed
a signed Spago cocktail napkin back to a fan.

"Not yet?" another photographer said. "Does that
mean you have plans to get married?"

Pierce smiled as if he had a great big happy secret.
"You'll be the first to know," he said, and put his arm
around Nikki's shoulders to steer her into the restaurant. "Excuse us, ladies and gentlemen, but we have
reservations for dinner." His smile turned deliciously
wicked. "A private celebration."

"Well," Nikki said a moment later as they sat down
at a corner table with a view of downtown Los Angeles, "that was certainly a masterful performance."

"Yes," Pierce said smugly. "Wasn't it?"

"NOBODY'S GOING TO BELIEVE we're sleeping together if you don't loosen up and move in a little closer," Pierce murmured into the feathery wisps of hair at Nikki's temple.

"Closer?" Nikki choked. "If I get any closer we're going to be wearing the same shirt."

Pierce grinned. "Sounds good to me." He tightened his arm around her waist, flexed his knees and swiveled his hips, dipping her backward with a sensual little movement that had her gasping for breath and grasping at his broad shoulders with both hands. "Now you're getting the hang of it," he murmured appreciatively, rocking her gently from side to side before he dipped down again.

They were dancing to Michael Bolton's "Save Me," their bodies plastered together on the crowded dance floor of a currently trendy Hollywood night spot. The lighting was low and intimate. The fake fog swirling around their feet was illuminated by sexy blue lights pulsating in time to the music as a man sang about being on fire with passion for the one woman who could save him.

Nikki had been struggling to think clearly from the minute Pierce took her into his arms and backed her onto the dance floor. But as his hands slid to her hips and his knee slipped between hers, she gave up the attempt as doomed to failure and gave in to pure primal feeling. Who needed to think when Pierce Kingston was crooning "'Lover, you've gotta save me,'" in your ear in a low, aching voice? Who *could* think? Certainly not her. Not when she was pressed from groin to breast to a man who had more moves than an L.A. Raider running back. Not when her heart was pounding in her ears loud enough to drown out the music and his was pounding against the aching tips of her breasts like a jackhammer gone wild. Not when she was on the verge of forgetting everything she'd ever learned about the futility of howling at the moon.

With what little was left of her mind, Nikki told herself that she was about to make the biggest mistake of her life. Bigger than yearning after unattainable football players in high school. Bigger than getting herself engaged to a hotshot pilot who was more interested in currying the influence of her father, Colonel Anthony Martinelli, than in teaching her about love.

Pierce Kingston was a rich, world-famous movie star who could have any woman he wanted. Who *had* had any woman he wanted, she reminded herself. He was spoiled and overindulged and, worst of all, he was acting.

And she *knew* he was acting.

They'd been building up to this all evening. In the restaurant over French champagne and designer pizza made of smoked salmon, caviar and *crème fraîche*, Pierce had looked at her with wicked, smoldering blue eyes and nibbled on her fingers between bites, giving the next day's tabloids something to write about. It was all an act.

So why did it feel so real? So right?

The music segued into "Now That I've Found You," the heartfelt, passionate ballad of a man who'd just found all he ever needed in the loving touch of a special woman. Nikki could feel Pierce's lips moving against her cheek, mouthing the words of the song. His hands were on her back, one low, fingers spread wide at the base of her spine, pressing her against his hardened body. The other was between her shoulder blades, under the long, sinuous strap of the small shoulder purse draped crosswise over her torso. He was rubbing his palm up and down, slowly caressing the length of her spine through the black silk of the Armani blouse he'd bought for her.

Nikki sighed and tightened her arms around his neck, threading the fingers of one hand through the thick golden hair that was inches longer than hers, and held on for dear life. They swayed slowly for a few long delicious moments more, rotating against each other, hips swiveling, melting together in the heat of the music and their own yearning bodies, melding their separate desires into one, torturing each other with a torrid simulation of the act they were both on fire for.

And then Pierce groaned, deep in his chest, and turned his head, nudging the corner of her mouth with his, seeking the taste of her. Helplessly, like a flower starved of moisture and sunlight, she turned her face up to his and opened her lips to his kiss.

They stopped dancing and stood there, an island of stillness in the middle of the crowded dance floor, kissing as if they were in the privacy of a secluded bedroom. His hands came up to cup her head. Hers fisted in his hair. Their heads tilted and turned, lips nibbling and tugging, tongues seeking. It was hot and wet and wild. And amazingly, incredibly sweet. And it went on forever, until, at last, Pierce tore his mouth away.

"Let's get the hell out of here before we get arrested," he growled, and dragged her from the dance floor.

THEY'D COOLED DOWN some by the time the car had been summoned and brought around to pick them up in front of the club. Enough so that Nikki kept her distance in the back of the limousine. Pierce sensed her nervousness and didn't press her, thinking it was the presence of the driver in the front seat that made her shy.

He didn't want her shy. He wanted her heated and avid and as hungry for him as he was for her, with no hesitation and no doubts, the way she had been those last few minutes on the dance floor. And for that he could wait. Not long, probably, he thought, looking at her shapely legs and her small breasts and the brave tilt of her vulnerable chin in the passing lights, but enough to get her into the privacy of his bedroom.

He intended to make love to her slowly, with every ounce of patience and skill he possessed. He wanted a long loving. A slow savoring. A banquet of the senses that would end with both of them sated and gasping for breath. He wanted to love her like no other man had ever loved her before. He wanted to possess her every thought and feeling. He wanted, he realized with a start of surprise, to bind her to him in the most basic way possible.

The realization came close to scaring him to death for a moment...until he managed to convince himself that he was allowing hormones to cloud his thought processes.

He wanted her.

Period.

There was nothing scary about that. He'd wanted dozens of women in his lifetime. Maybe not as badly as he wanted Nikki Martinelli, but it was really only a matter of degree. And the cure for that wanting was in having. Soon. He leaned over and put his lips next to her ear.

"When I get you upstairs," he whispered as the long black car turned into the driveway. "I'm going to peel you out of that sexy little miniskirt and that silk blouse and whatever else you have on, and lick every inch of those gorgeous legs of yours," he said in a low, heated voice, "starting with your toes."

Nikki turned her head sharply, looking at him with a wide-eyed, shocked expression, as if she'd never in her life heard of such a thing but thought it sounded awfully interesting. And then she blushed—a deep red blush that began under the collar of her blouse and flooded her whole face with rosy color.

Pierce was utterly entranced. "Wait until I tell you about some of the other things we're going to do together," he promised, giving her his pirate's grin. "Your whole body will turn red. If it hasn't already."

She was out of the limousine and to the top of the front stairs before Pierce had tipped the driver and sent him on his way.

"You can't get in without me," Pierce said, hurrying up the steps behind her. He held something up between his thumb and forefinger. "I have the key. Although," he added, as he fit it into the lock, "you could probably go around back and get in through the garden room. Or my bedroom. I'm pretty sure I left the glass doors open." He pushed the door open and ushered her into the dark, shadowed foyer. "I usually do."

"That's not putting your security system to very good use," Nikki chided.

Pierce smiled at her. "I don't have a security system except for the one that guards the paintings." He reached out to touch her nose with his fingertip. "And you, of course."

Nikki ducked his hand and backed away.

He dropped his hand without touching her. "What's the matter, Nikki?"

"Nothing," she said quickly. "Everything. Oh, God." She turned away from him. "I feel like such a fool."

He felt a terrible sense of foreboding. "Tell me," he said, hoping she wasn't going to say what he thought she was going to say.

But she did.

"I know I gave you the impression that I—that I wanted to make...ah...wanted to go to bed with you. And I do," she admitted wretchedly. "But I shouldn't."

"Shouldn't?"

"Because of who you are. Because of who I am. I hardly know you, really. And you're technically my boss. And what happened between us tonight was just—" she waved her hands a bit frantically "—just for show. To draw your fan out. I know that. And yet I still—"

"No," Pierce said. "It wasn't."

"Wasn't?"

"For show. I wanted you. *Want* you," he corrected himself. "I'd never pretend about a thing like that." There was a beat of silence as he looked at her. "I'd think you would have been able to tell."

"Oh, well, physically, yes, I could tell that, but . . ." She was blushing again. "It isn't enough." *It never had been for her,* she thought. But if he pushed at all, she might very well decide that it was. And that would be disastrous.

She waited a minute for him to push her.

"I think I'd better just go to my room," she said, at last. "Alone."

"If you feel that way, then I guess you should," Pierce said gently. He didn't have any arguments to counter her charge that it was just physical between them, because it *was* just physical. Mostly physical, anyway. Wasn't it?

"You don't mind?"

"I mind like hell," he admitted, "but it's your decision."

"Then, I guess I'll go." She backed up a few steps, her black stiletto heels clicking on the polished marble floor, then paused uncertainly. "You'll remember to close your patio doors, won't you?"

He nodded.

"And lock them."

He nodded again.

"Well," she said, her gaze skittering around the quiet foyer as she searched for something else to say to prolong the moment.

"Nikki." He waited until she looked at him. "If you're going to go to your room—alone—then I suggest you go," he said in a low, tense voice, "before I forget I'm a gentleman and take the choice out of your hands."

Her eyes widened at his tone. "Good night, then," she gulped.

"Good night, Nikki." He watched her turn and run all the way up the wide curving stairway to the second floor while he stood in the foyer below and fought the urge to throw back his head and howl with disappointment and frustration.

7

NIKKI LAY IN THE BIG tester bed under the puffy-green-and-ivory-leaf-strewn comforter, telling herself to just forget what might have been and go to sleep. After a long, agonizing hour of tossing and turning, she kicked the comforter to the foot of the bed and gave it up as a lost cause. There was no way she was getting any sleep tonight. Not as long as "what might have been" was in the very next room.

She wondered how he slept, there in the bed in the very next room. Did he curl up on his side, like she did? Or was he a sprawler? Did he pull the covers up under his chin or kick them to the floor? Did he wear tailored black silk pajamas or go to bed gloriously naked? Did he snore? Did he talk in his sleep?

And had he remembered to close and lock his door like she'd told him to?

She lay there for a moment longer, fighting the urge, telling herself it was none of her business, that he was a grown man who could sleep with his bedroom doors open if he wanted to.

Damn it, she thought, *it is my business.* She was his bodyguard. And if he wouldn't take the few simple steps necessary to protect himself . . . well, it was up to her to do it for him. That's what she'd been hired for.

"I'll just get up and check," she said to herself as she swung her bare legs over the side of the bed. "That's all. I'll do a quick check and then come right back to bed."

She slid from the bed and tiptoed through the darkened bedroom, guided only by the moonlight shining in through the multipaned glass doors. Quietly, with her left hand pressed against the door frame to minimize noise, she turned the ornate, old-fashioned handle slowly until it opened with a soft snick. It sounded like a cannon shot in the dark stillness of the night. Nikki sucked in her breath and waited for something—anything—to happen. When nothing did, she slowly pulled the door the rest of the way open and stepped out onto the stone terrace.

It was a perfect night, warm and sweet, with the smell of bougainvillea and roses and night-blooming jasmine perfuming the air. The moonlight reflected off the water in the swimming pool below. A soft breeze was blowing, tugging at the hem of Nikki's extra large, marine-issue green T-shirt, making it ripple against her thighs. She tiptoed past the wrought-iron patio furniture without giving it a glance, headed toward the double-glass doors to Pierce's bedroom.

They were wide open.

Nikki halted in indecision.

If he was asleep, would she wake him by closing them? And, if he was awake, would he read something other than professional concern for his safety into her actions? She tiptoed closer...a step...two...until she was standing in the open doorway. She leaned forward, peering into the darkness of his room. "Pierce?" she whispered, too low for anyone who was sleeping to hear her.

There was no answer.

How on earth can he be sleeping? she wondered indignantly.

Here she was, unable to close her eyes, all tangled up inside with frustrated passion and wildly confused emotions—and he was sleeping like an innocent baby! She had half a mind to wake him up and tell him just what she thought of his callous, uncaring behavior. She took a step forward, halfway intending to do just that.

"Planning to murder me in my sleep?" said a voice from behind her.

Nikki whirled around as if she'd been shot, her hand going up to her mouth to cover a squeak of surprise. He was sitting at the patio table in his familiar loose-limbed slouch, barefoot, bare chested, in a pair of soft old sweatpants with the drawstring waist riding low on his nonexistent hips. "Pierce, what in heaven's name are you doing out here in the middle of the night?" she demanded peevishly, aghast at being caught hovering around his bedroom door.

"I could ask you the same question."

"I was just checking," she said quickly, "to, ah . . . to see if you'd closed and locked your doors like I told you to."

He gave her a knowing look. "Uh-huh."

"Well, I was."

"Uh-huh," he said again, letting her know he wasn't fooled in the least by her flimsy excuse. He gestured at the squat green bottle on the glass-topped table in front of him. "Care to join me in a drink?"

Nikki tiptoed a few steps closer. "What is it?" she asked, trying not to stare at his bare, hairy chest. It looked a mile wide and as hard as sculpted marble in the moonlight.

"Armagnac. Fifty-year-old Armagnac." He took a healthy swallow from the oversized snifter he held cradled in his hand. "Good for what ails you."

Nikki reached out and touched her fingertips to the high arched back of one of the wrought-iron chairs. "And what ails you?" she asked quietly.

Pierce snorted and gave her an incredulous look.

"Yeah, me, too," she admitted, surprising them both with her candidness. She pulled the chair away from the table and plopped down into it. "Sexual frustration is hell, isn't it?" she said forlornly, like a child who'd just discovered that sad fact.

Pierce very nearly smiled. "Indeed it is," he agreed. He held the snifter out to her. "Sip?"

She took the oversized balloon-shaped glass in both hands and brought it to her nose to sniff. "Does it help?"

"No," he said, watching her tongue flicker out to taste the fiery liquid before committing herself to anything more. Nikki Martinelli was a cautious woman. Why was he only just realizing that?

She looked at him over the rim of the glass. "Does anything?" she asked seriously, as if she really wanted to know. "Help, I mean?"

"Only giving in to what ails you in the first place," he said bluntly, fighting the urge to show her just exactly what *would* help.

Nikki put the drink down onto the table between them, untasted. "I'm sorry," she said. "I didn't mean to get you all . . . riled up and then—" what was it her brothers always said? "—and then not come across with the goods. I know how men feel about a tease." Which was why she'd never let herself get into a situation where she could be accused of teasing. Until now.

"It isn't teasing if you mean it," Pierce said gently, feeling guilty for making her feel guilty. "Even if you change your mind later." He ran a fingertip around the rim of the snifter, concentrating on the repetitive motion in an effort to keep his eyes off her legs. "Besides, I'd say it worked both ways tonight." He looked at her from under his lashes, one corner of his mouth lifted in a wry smile. "You did imply you were suffering from some degree of sexual frustration yourself."

"Well, yes," Nikki admitted, staring at his slowly circling finger. "But it's my own fault. You were willing to—" she licked her lower lip "—to, ah . . ."

Pierce smiled. "Come across with the goods?"

"Yes," she said breathlessly.

"I still am," he said simply. "Now. A week from now. A month from now." He leaned back in his chair, deliberately casual and nonthreatening. If a first move was going to be made tonight, she would have to make it. "Whenever you're ready."

She just looked at him, helplessly, not knowing what to do or say.

Sensing her confusion, touched by it, he reached out and covered her hand with his where it lay on the table. "It's become very apparent to me that I tried to push you too far, too fast. You're not a woman who rushes into things. You need time to get to know me. To feel comfortable with me. To get used to being touched by me in a casual way before you commit yourself to anything more. That's nothing to feel guilty about. Hell," he said, and squeezed her hand, "in this day and age, that's a laudable approach to intimacy."

"That's not the reason I said no," she said, staring at his hand on hers. "Not the main reason, anyway. Mainly, I said no because—" she shrugged "—well, partially because you're my boss. And partially because you're who you are. I meant what I said earlier about not standing in line." She drew her hand out from under his and clasped both hers together in her lap to keep from reaching for him. "But mostly because . . ."

"Because?" Pierce prompted.

"There's something you should know about me," she said.

Pierce sat quietly, waiting for her to go on, wondering what terrible thing she was about to confess. From the look on her face it had to be something serious.

Nikki took a deep breath and lifted her gaze to his. There was no easy way to say, "I'm a sucker for a pretty face," she said, as if admitting to a strong liking for kinky sex acts.

Relief flooded through him. "And?" he prompted, trying to keep his lips from twitching.

"I'm . . . drawn to good-looking men, I guess you could say. I know it's shallow of me. That it's superficial. And stupid, considering all the grief they've given me. But I can't seem to help it. Every guy I've ever been attracted to has been good-looking. Not nearly as good looking as you," she added honestly, letting her gaze drift over his face for a moment. "But more than commonly attractive." She shrugged and looked down at her lap again. "I think it's probably some kind of Freudian complex or something. My father and all my brothers are big, good looking men, especially when they're all decked out in their navy whites. All the guys I had unrequited crushes on in every high school I ever went to were good-looking, too. And my fiancé was a walking, talking navy recruiting poster."

"And he cheated on you."

That brought her gaze up to his. "How did you know?"

"The remark you made about not standing in line for any man again." He shrugged. "It wasn't difficult to figure out." He looked at the top of her bent head. "Want to tell me about it?"

"There's not much to tell. I fell head over heels in love with a pretty face and he fell head over heels in love with my father's rank and what he thought it could do for him. End of story."

"Hardly." Pierce's voice was dry and disbelieving.

"No, that's pretty much it," Nikki said. "The rest is the old familiar tale of a woman scorned. I went over to his apartment one afternoon with a picnic lunch, a surprise to welcome him home from an extended training mission." She gave a short mirthless little laugh. "The surprise was on me."

"He was with another woman."

"Yes. Buck naked and thrashing around on the living room floor in the final throes of ecstasy."

"It must have hurt."

"Like hell," Nikki admitted. "Especially since he'd refused to make love to *me*. I'd shown him in every way I knew how that I was willing to sleep with him anytime he wanted me, but he said he wanted to do everything right, to wait until the wedding night, and I'd agreed because I thought it was so romantic and gallant of him. The truth was that he was afraid my father or one of my brothers would find out if he took me to bed before the ceremony and it would ruin his chances for a fast promotion. Bump him right off the fast track. He didn't want me enough to risk it."

"The fool." Pierce's voice was scathing.

"No, he was right, it probably would have affected his career. The men in my family are stereotypical Italians when it comes to their women. Any one of them would have squashed him like a bug if they thought he'd taken advantage of me."

"So did you ruin him instead?"

"No. I told my family I'd changed my mind about getting married and ran off to join the marines."

"And vowed never to trust another good-looking man again as long as you lived."

"And vowed never to trust *myself* with another good-looking man as long as I lived," Nikki corrected him.

Pierce looked at her for a long, thoughtful moment, wondering what he could say to convince her that she could trust herself to him, especially when he wasn't sure she could, completely. "I'd never cheat on you," he said at last, because it was the only promise he could make. He reached out and touched her cheek, stroking it gently with the backs of his fingers. "And I want you enough to risk anything, even the wrath of your menfolk." His fingers drifted under her chin, lifting it. "The question is, do you want me enough to take a few risks of your own?"

And that, Nikki thought, staring into his eyes, *is the sixty-four thousand dollar question*. Did she want him enough to cast aside all her doubts and hesitations? Did she want him enough to take another chance on getting hurt? She took a shaky breath. "Yes," she said, realizing as she said it that it was truer than anything had ever been. She wanted him enough to risk anything.

"I'm not promising you a lifetime of tomorrows, or some rosy happily ever after," he warned her, compelled to be brutally honest. "I don't have that in me. But I am promising complete faithfulness while we're together. If that isn't enough, well—" he let his hand drop from her face "—then I'll back off now."

Nikki reached out and captured the hand that had been caressing her face. "It's enough," she said, and brought it to her T-shirt covered breast.

Pierce's breath hissed inward with excitement, but he controlled himself. He curled his fingers very gently around her softness. "You're sure?" he murmured.

"Yes," she said fiercely, closing her eyes against the pleasure of his touch. "Yes."

"You don't want to wait to get to know me a little better first?"

She opened her eyes. "Not unless you do," she began uncertainly, and Pierce could see the self-doubt building in her eyes.

Cursing himself for his clumsiness, Pierce surged to his feet and pulled her out of the chair and into his arms. One big hand curved over her tight little buttocks, pressing her lower body against the granite hardness of his loins. "I don't even want to wait to get you into bed." He growled the words into her ear. "But I think I can manage to restrain myself until then. Barely," he said, bending down to swoop her up into his arms.

He carried her across the stone terrace and through the open doors into his bedroom. She felt the tangled sheets under her back—evidence of his previous restlessness—as he laid her on the bed. And then his body came down on top of hers, pressing her into the mattress, and all she could feel was him.

He forgot his promise to himself to go slowly as her arms came up around his neck. He forgot about savoring and feasting and prolonging consummation until they were both crazy for it. All he could think about, now, with her soft and sweet and yielding beneath him, was the driving need for immediate possession.

He covered her mouth with his, roughly, thrusting his tongue between her lips, demanding immediate entrance. His hands skimmed along her sides, grasping her hips to pull her more fully under him, then smoothing down her thighs to the backs of her knees, lifting them high so he could settle himself more firmly between her legs. He thrust against her heavily, in fevered simulation of the act to come. Instinctively, wanting him even closer, she locked her ankles across the small of his back and lifted her hips into the blatantly carnal caress. He groaned, deep in his chest, and pushed himself up onto his elbows so he could look down at her.

"I fantasized about this from the minute I saw you," he said raggedly, holding her head cradled in his palms. "You, under me, with your gorgeous legs wrapped around my waist." He pressed soft, openmouthed kisses over her face as he slowly rotated his hips against the apex of her thighs. "I promised to lick every inch of your legs . . . remember?"

Her lips trembled against his. "I remember," she said.

"And I will," he promised hoarsely. "Later." He kissed her again, hotly, deeply, his fingers spread in the short feathery layers of her silky hair, his thumbs stroking the delicate underside of her jaw, his mouth open wide over hers, as if he meant to consume her. They were both breathing hard when he lifted his head again. "Right now, I just want to be inside you. I need to be inside you," he confessed gruffly, his voice thick with passion. He reached down as he spoke, catching the hem of her T-shirt in his hands, dragging it up and over her head. "Let's get this off."

Nikki helped him, arching her back, lifting her shoulders, raising her arms to facilitate the garment's removal. It was nothing but a barrier to what she wanted with every fiber of her being. She reached down as he tossed the T-shirt away, hooking her thumbs in the elastic of her panties, frantically trying to wriggle out of them.

He levered himself up off her body, rolling to the side to rid himself of his own remaining garment. He kicked his sweatpants to the floor and reached for her, one arm sliding under her shoulders to hold her close, the other hand reaching for the treasure hidden between her legs. Her hips bucked when he touched the slick wet heat of her and she grabbed his upper arms, biting down on her bottom lip to hold back a whimper as he gently probed her body's most delicate folds. The whimper escaped as he inserted one long finger into her, and she tensed, her heels pressing into the mattress, her body going as stiff as a board. He withdrew, then entered her again, even more gently than before, going a bit deeper this time. Her whimper turned to a little gasping pant, a sound that was half primal feminine fear, half unbearable excitement. Her hands tightened on his arms, her fingers digging into the rock-hard muscles of his biceps as she waited for him to take the next step.

Pierce stilled and withdrew his hand, letting it rest on the soft triangle of silky black hair between her thighs. He took a deep, shaky breath, and then another, his chest heaving like a bellows, before he could draw in enough air to speak. "I think there's a little something you neglected to mention."

"It's nothing," Nikki panted. She released her death grip on one arm and reached down to take his wrist, trying to push his hand back between her legs. "It's not important."

"It *is* important." He moved the wrist she was tugging on, bringing his hand up under her chin to lift her face to his. "Nikki," he said, peering down at her in the dim light with a look of infinite tenderness on his handsome face, "why didn't you tell me you're a virgin?"

She was silent for a long moment, her eyes closed, her hand still clinging to his wrist, fervently praying he wouldn't see her embarrassment. "Does it matter?" she said at last.

"Only in how we go about this."

She opened her eyes. "Does that mean you still want to?"

"Good God, yes." He hugged her to him with the arm under her shoulders, giving her a quick, hard, possessive kiss. *How on earth can she think I don't want to?* "Yes. More than ever."

"More than ever?" she asked, puzzled.

"Do you have the faintest idea what it does to a man to find out he's the first?" His lips turned up in a wry, self-deprecating smile as she gazed up at him without answering. "No, I guess you don't. Well—" he ran a fingertip down the long elegant line of her throat as he spoke "—let's just say it appeals to all his less-evolved, baser male instincts and let it go at that."

Nikki managed to lift a delicate eyebrow. "His?"

Pierce grinned his pirate's grin. "All right. Mine," he acknowledged, skimming his finger over the soft skin of her upper chest, down between her breasts to her navel, smiling wolfishly as her skin quivered in response. "It appeals to all *my* less-evolved, baser male instincts," he said as he outlined the silky triangle of hair at the base of her abdomen. "All those testosterone-fueled instincts civilization has supposedly bred out of the male animal but really hasn't." He flattened his hand over her mound in a blatantly possessive gesture, as if to show her what he meant, and bent his head to kiss her. "How'd I get so lucky?" he murmured against her lips.

"Lucky?"

"Not many women in this day and age are still virgins at . . . what?" He lifted his head to look at her. "Twenty-three? Twenty-four?"

"Twenty-four," she muttered shortly, and tried to draw his mouth back down to hers before he could pursue the subject any further.

He resisted. "Why?"

"I don't want to talk about it."

"Why, Nikki?"

"I really don't think it's any of your business." She gave him a narrow look meant to discourage further inquiries. "Unless you're willing to answer a few questions about your past in return," she added, thinking that would make him back off.

"I'll answer any questions about my sex life you'd care to ask," he said, "*after* you answer mine."

She clamped her lips together, unwilling to tell him why she was still a virgin at the advanced age of twenty-four. It made her sound so . . . pathetic.

"Why, Nikki?"

"Because nobody ever asked me, that's why," she burst out finally, realizing he wasn't going to let it go until he had an answer. "Because I've always been so tall and skinny and . . . and socially inept that no one ever wanted me." She turned her head, not wanting to see the pity on his face.

Pierce was silent for a stunned moment, trying to make sense of what she'd said. *No one wanted her? Was she crazy? How could she think any man could look at her and not want her?* It made absolutely no sense for her to— "Those unrequited crushes in high school," he muttered, as understanding slowly dawned. "And that idiot fiancé of yours." He nodded to himself. "Okay, I'll buy that. You were one of those gangly, awkward teenagers. A foot taller than all the guys, right? And probably painfully shy because of it." He smiled tenderly as he pictured it in his mind's eye. "I can see how that might have limited your romantic experience when you were a teenager. But what about later?"

"Later?" she said, without looking at him.

"Last I heard, the Marine Corps was full of men. Don't tell me none of them ever asked you."

"Military life is easier if you're just one of the guys." Nikki shrugged against the pillow. "And I've been one of the guys all my life."

Pierce snorted in disbelief. "Some guy," he said, and slid his hand between her thighs to emphasize his point.

Nikki caught her breath and lifted her gaze to his. Did this mean he still wanted—

"I want you more than ever," he said, answering her unasked question.

Nikki shivered with a combination of delight and arousal and a sort of fearful anticipation and reached up to twine her arms around his neck. Their lips met in a soft, sweet, deliciously warm kiss that seemed to last for days, and then Pierce pulled away gently, kissing her cheeks and eyelids and the palm of each hand as he unwrapped her arms from around his neck.

"What I'd like to do is fall on you like a hungry hound," he said, giving her a look that left no doubt in her mind about the truth of his statement, "but a woman's first time should be extra special." He rose from the bed. "You wait right here while I see what I can do to make it that way."

"You don't have to do any—"

He put a fingertip to her lips, stopping her. "I want to," he said, his eyes blazing with passion and tenderness as he stared down at her. He leaned down and kissed her again. "Don't move a muscle until I get back."

Nikki disobeyed him, sitting up and reaching for the sheet as he turned away. She pulled it over her breasts and lay back down, smiling mistily as she watched him move around the room, deliberately setting the scene for her deflowering.

He was glorious in his nudity. Utterly unselfconscious and more perfect than any man ever made. His shoulders were wide and rounded with muscle, his back was broad and smooth, the deep cleft of his spine dividing it neatly in half. His hips were narrow, his buttocks tight, his legs long and lean, the thighs as hard and muscled as any professional athlete's.

He went to the fieldstone fireplace opposite the bed first and set a match to the kindling and logs that were always stacked in readiness, then lit the half-a-dozen candles placed all around the room, bathing them in the warm golden glow of firelight. Opening a huge seventeenth-century oak armoire, he rummaged through a vast collection of compact discs until he found the one he wanted. In just a few minutes, the same artist they had danced to in the club began to sing softly about love and passion. Quickly, then, he moved to air-conditioning controls, adjusting them to compensate for the warmth being generated by the fireplace, then crossed over to the open glass doors. After closing them, he pulled the sheer under curtains together to shut out the night.

"Now, my dear," he said, turning back to Nikki with a mock leer, "I have you at my mercy."

Nikki gulped, trying not to stare at his erection, and instinctively clutched the sheet more closely to her breasts.

"You moved," he accused as he approached the foot of the bed. "Naughty girl," he chided, shaking his finger at her. "I told you not to move." He reached out and took the sheet in his fist. "Do you know what I do to naughty little girls who disobey me?"

Eyes wide and shining with excitement and anticipation, Nikki shook her head against the pillow.

He tugged on the sheet, silently demanding that she release it, dragging it, inch by inch, down her supine body, teasing them both with the slow unveiling of her feminine charms. "I drive them insane with desire," he said as he pulled it over the hard, pebbled tips of her breasts. "I make them crazy with lust and passion." He drew the sheet lower, down over her flat little stomach and the soft flare of her hips. "I make them delirious with need," he promised as the soft percale brushed over the silky black hair at the base of her abdomen and the long, sleek muscles of her thighs before exposing her rounded knees and the smooth skin of her calves and the delicate bones of her feet. "I make them beg for mercy," he said, and dropped the bunched material to the floor.

"Please," Nikki whispered in a choked voice.

Pierce leaned over and grasped her ankle. "I think I'll start here," he said evilly, and bent his head to kiss the tip of her big toe.

Nikki gasped and her foot jerked in his hand.

He held her firmly, intent on doing as he'd promised and caressing every inch of her long, gorgeous legs with his mouth. Intent, too, on impressing upon her just how lovely he found her long, lanky body. He kissed her insteps and nipped at her ankles. He ran his lips over her calves and nibbled on her knees and took little cat licks all along the smooth skin of her thighs. And all the while he whispered to her, murmuring hot, breathless accolades to the unique beauty of her long legs and the special silkiness of her skin. And then, finally, on his stomach between her thighs, he pushed them apart and draped them over his shoulders. Opening her soft, feminine folds with his fingertips, he bent his head to give her the most intimate kiss of all.

Nikki gave a muffled shriek and fisted her hands in his hair, squirming and panting, pleading incoherently with him to please stop . . . and to never stop. She shrieked again, long sweet moments later, writhing helplessly when she climaxed for the first time.

"Please," she said breathlessly, trying to pull his tormenting mouth away from her body by tugging on his hair. "Please, Pierce, you're making me crazy."

"I want you crazy," he murmured into the soft skin of her thigh. "It's good when you're crazy," he said, but he let her pull him slowly higher, planting numerous moist, openmouthed kisses on her stomach and ribs until, finally, he reached the quivering mounds of her breasts. They were incredibly soft and delicate under his lips, topped with small rosy nipples, drawn tight with need. "Beautiful," he murmured as he cupped them in his big hands. "Perfect." Plumping them up, he bent his head to taste them more fully.

Nikki sighed and gentled her hands in his hair, curving her fingers around his skull to hold him to her, silently urging him to take his fill as she smoothed the damp golden curls that fell over his ears and caressed his strong neck. He let her drift for a moment or two, let her luxuriate in the orgasm he'd just given her, let her savor his lavish attention to her breasts. And then he took one tight little nipple into his mouth and bit it gently.

Nikki moaned and arched up off the bed. "Please," she said again, hardly knowing what she was saying. "Please, Pierce, I need . . ."

He lifted his head and looked at her, his blue eyes gleaming with lust and other, more complicated, emotions. "What?" he murmured. "What do you need?"

"You," she said. "I need you. Inside me. Now. Please. I don't want to wait any longer."

"Neither do I," he whispered, and gently disengaged himself from her clinging arms to reach for the condoms stored in his nightstand. He lifted himself away from her to deal with it and then, only seconds later, eased himself back between her thighs. "Now," he said softly, and took her wrists in his hands. He pushed them down, flat against the mattress on either side of her head. "Look at me, Nikki," he commanded, his voice low and rasping.

She stared up at him, her gaze locked on his as he slid his palms up over hers and threaded their fingers together.

"Mine," he said as he slowly began to enter her.

She felt his shaft probing at the wet, heated entrance to her body, pushing at the fragile barrier of her virginity, and she arched up to meet it, head-on, gasping just a bit as he broke through and filled her to the hilt.

"Okay?" he murmured raggedly, determined not to move until she was ready for more.

It took a moment or two for her to get used to the feel of him inside her—a moment or two when his body trembled violently and he thought he would die from the strain of holding back—and then she smiled and sighed.

"Yes," she said, her pale green eyes glowing with satisfaction and surrender and a sense of wonder that anything could feel so good. "Yes."

"Yes," he echoed, his eyes reflecting the same sense of satisfaction that shone in hers, as well as a particularly masculine blend of triumph and possession. "Oh, yes."

He began to move, slowly at first and then faster as she started to breath more rapidly, responding to him with soft cries and gasps, meeting each of his thrusts with one of her own. Finally their bodies were rocking in unconscious time to the music that pulsated through the room, moving together in the oldest dance of all. Pierce groaned loudly at the end, holding her slender body tight against him as he stiffened in release. Nikki's second explosive climax of the evening was underscored by the joyous sound of Michael Bolton singing "Love Is A Wonderful Thing" and her lover breathing the word "mine" over and over in her ear.

8

PIERCE TENSED, breathing out through his mouth as he slowly flexed the powerful muscles of his shoulders and chest and straightened his elbows. He did it eleven more times, moving just as slowly and powerfully as he had the first time, regulating his breathing to coincide with his movements, until finally, he straightened his arms completely and returned the weighted bar to the rack above his head. He levered himself to a sitting position, one foot on either side of the narrow weight bench, and wiped his face with the towel he'd slung around his neck, wondering if he was going to be so masochistic as to force himself to finish the entire routine when what he really wanted to do was go back to his room and crawl into bed with Nikki.

And not just to make love to her again, either, he told himself virtuously.

Not that he didn't want to, Lord knew. Even after having made tempestuous, tumultuous, body-and-soul satisfying love to her three times in as many hours, he was still edgy and half-aroused and more than ready to rise to the occasion at the slightest encouragement.

Or with no encouragement at all.

Which was why he was out in the cabana weight room at three o'clock in the morning, in sweatpants and high-tops, doing his damnedest to work himself into a state of utter exhaustion before going back to bed. "To sleep," he reminded himself as his unruly body began to stir to life at the mere thought of the warm, tousled woman in his bed.

She'd been sleeping deeply when he left her, curled up on her side like an exhausted child with her hands tucked under her chin, the covers pulled over her shoulders and her short feathery hair sticking up in all directions. He could probably slide into bed without even waking her, he thought longingly, just snuggle right up to her warm, lithesome body and hold her while she slept, her back to his front, like spoons. He hadn't made love to her that way, yet....

"Jeez, Kingston," he muttered, disgusted with himself and his rampaging libido. "What the hell's the matter with you? You haven't been this horny since..."

He honestly couldn't remember the last time. When he'd first reached puberty, probably, and constant thoughts of sex and girls had kept him in a perpetual state of arousal. But not since then, certainly. Women were just too available to him, to eager and willing, for him to get into much of a swelter over any one in particular. He'd always been like the proverbial honeybee, flitting from flower to flower, enjoying and being enjoyed, with no thought of anything permanent or lasting.

Until now.

Until now, he hadn't even considered the possibility of anything permanent. Or even semipermanent. He was too much like his father, everyone always said, too much the debonair ladies' man, too much the gallant, lighthearted lover to ever tie himself to just one woman. Except that he didn't feel lighthearted now.

He felt...possessive. Proprietary. Greedy. *Mine*, he'd said as he slipped into the incredible heat and tightness of her. *Mine*, he'd said as her hips rolled beneath him and she made those breathless little panting noises in his ear. *Mine*, he'd said when she gasped out his name and came apart in his arms. And the really scary thing was that, on some basic, primitive, heretofore untapped level of his masculine psyche, he'd meant it. Literally. Like a stallion who'd cut a mare out of the herd, he'd claimed her, marking her as his own with his possession of her body, and now she was *his*.

He'd never felt that way about a woman before. Ever.

And it scared him spitless that he felt that way now.

He tried to tell himself that it had to have something to do with the fact that she'd been a virgin. *A virgin!* he thought, shaking his head with the wonder of it. He'd never made love to a virgin before. His own first experience had been at the hands of an experienced twenty-three-year old starlet who'd played his older sister in one of his early films. But it stood to reason that being the first man to possess a woman's body would affect his feelings for her in some weird way. That it would stir up some ancient, primitive ownership instincts or something. It was the only explanation for the way he was feeling.

Because the way he was feeling was . . . crazy.

He wasn't equipped for the long-term. Like his father, he lacked whatever it was that was so necessary for permanent bonding with a woman and, unlike his father, he knew it. He wasn't about to risk ruining a woman's life by offering her any sort of permanence in a fit of testosterone-induced ardor that rarely lasted beyond a few heated months. Because, no matter how hot the fire seemed in the beginning, it *always* ended.

Usually he viewed the inevitable termination of an affair with equanimity and the careless sangfroid of a man who knew there would always be another woman. But this wasn't "usually," he thought uneasily. It wasn't anything like "usually."

It was ... visceral.

All-consuming.

Intense.

And, for a man whose deepest feelings had never really been engaged before, frightening in a way that he couldn't articulate or explain.

Pierce reacted the way most men do to vague fears, unexplainable emotions and frustrated passion—with aggression. He jumped up from the weight bench, yanked the towel from around his neck and attacked the body bag as if it were a living adversary to be subdued. He leaned in close, hunching his shoulders, aiming his punches at what would have been a human opponent's vulnerable midsection. Two left jabs...a right cross...all delivered with a bouncing step that kept the laces on his high-topped athletic shoes swaying as he moved his feet in a pattern as intricate as any dance steps. He settled into a punishing routine intended to exhaust his superbly conditioned body and empty his mind of everything except what he was doing.

And then, suddenly, a shrill sound, as grating as fingernails on a blackboard, ripped through early-morning darkness with a pulsating whine that demanded immediate attention. Pierce checked himself in midpunch, his head jerking toward the sound, his feet already carrying him toward the open door of the cabana to investigate. He was moving at a slow lope as he rounded the pool and flower beds, his eyes searching the massive stone structure for any indication of what—or who—had caused the alarm to go off. He saw lights come on. Heard women's voices raised in fear and confusion. And realized, suddenly, exactly what the shrieking alarm was warning them of.

"Nikki," he mouthed frantically, breaking into a run as he reached the terrace steps. Black smoke was billowing out of his open bedroom doors. "*Nikki!*"

THE SCREAMING ALARM jerked Nikki from a deep, dreamless sleep, catapulting her into a waking nightmare of noise and heat and confusion. Her eyes stung fiercely as she struggled to open them, and every breath she dragged into her heaving lungs burned all the way down. Flames flickered through the smoke, as deadly and threatening as living monsters as they crawled across the carpet. She stared at them in confusion for a moment, her mind disoriented by smoke and sleep. And then, realizing what was happening, she scrambled up, coughing and choking, and flung an arm to the side to rouse her lover and warn him of the danger.

"Pierce," she croaked hoarsely, blindly searching for him among the tumbled covers. Smoke-induced tears streamed down her face as she scrambled, naked, on all fours over the bed, trying to find him. "*Pierce!*" she screamed frantically, the word no more than a rasp of sound in her smoke-clogged throat.

She grabbed a pillow and rolled off the bed, intending to beat a path through the smoldering carpet and free him from the flames. It was her duty to watch over him, she thought frantically. Her duty to see that no harm came to him while he was in her charge. He was her responsibility. Hers to protect and care for. *Hers*. And she had failed him.

"*Pierce! Where are you?*"

Something clamped around her bare waist, lifting her off her feet and yanking her back away from the danger of the flames licking around her ankles. She kicked backward, instinctively using the side of her foot in a determined effort to free herself. There was a grunt of pain as it connected with something solid. The clamp around her waist faltered and then tightened painfully, lifting her even further off of her feet.

"Nikki." The word was low and intense and spoken right next to her ear. "Nikki, it's me. Pierce. We've got to get out of here."

"The fire—"

"The hell with the fire," he said, awkwardly dragging her backward. "The fire is nothing. It's the smoke we've got to worry about. We've got to get out of here. *Now.*"

The sense of what he was saying got through to her then. She dropped the pillow and stopped struggling to get away, struggling instead to get to her feet and drag *him* to safety.

" . . . get you out of here," she muttered purposefully, wrapping an arm around his waist to assist him from the room.

They stumbled out of the bedroom and onto the terrace together, weaving like a pair of drunks on a binge, tears streaming down their faces from the sharp sting of the smoke. Other hands reached for them as they started down the stone stairway to the ground below, offering support as they took the last few tottering steps toward safety.

"Oh, my God, Oh, my God, are you all right?"

"Mr. Kingston, what happened?"

"Are either of you hurt? Is anyone burned?"

Pierce ignored the questions. "Someone call the fire department," he bellowed, raising his voice over the sound of the fire alarm that still screamed inside the house. His arms tightened around Nikki, shielding and supporting her against his chest as she took deep, heaving gulps of sweet, clean air into her lungs. "And get Nikki something to put on."

"I've already called 911," Kathy said, stripping off her blue silk peignoir as she spoke. Pierce grabbed it from her without a word. "You can hear the sirens already," she said, watching as he tenderly wrapped it around his bodyguard's naked, trembling form.

"I thought you were caught in the fire," Nikki said, her voice barely more than a hoarse whisper. She clung to him, resisting his efforts to guide her arms into the borrowed robe. "I thought you were hurt." Her hands skimmed frantically over his shoulders and chest, as if checking for damage. "Or dying. When I couldn't find you I thought—"

"I'm all right," he said, abandoning his efforts at dressing her to pull her tight against his chest. Nikki gasped, coughing, and wrapped her arms around his waist, burying her face in the warm curve of his neck. He cupped the back of her head in his hand and held her there, pressing his cheek against her hair. "*We're* all right," he said, soothing them both with the close contact of their bodies and the faint rocking motion one uses to calm a baby.

They stood like that for a long moment, holding on tight, each physically affirming that the other was alive and breathing and safe, until, finally, the sound of screaming sirens became louder than the din of the fire alarm, announcing the arrival of the Beverly Hills fire department.

"Lisbeth, run around front and tell them the fire's back here so they don't tear down the front door and tromp all through the house looking for it," Pierce ordered over Nikki's head.

The girl just stood there in her yellow Snoopy nightshirt, staring at Pierce and Nikki with a flabbergasted look on her face, as if she couldn't believe her eyes.

"Go," he said sternly, and Lisbeth fled to do his bidding.

Nikki drew back out of Pierce's embrace and slipped her arms into the wide kimono sleeves of the borrowed robe, suddenly embarrassed at her nakedness and the reason for it and the way she'd exposed her feelings to everyone watching.

"You look like a chimney sweep," Pierce said, his smile tender and teasing as he helped her pull the edges of the silky robe together. His fingers drifted upward to touch her cheek. "You have soot all over your face." He smoothed the hair at her temple. "And your hair's sticking up all over your head."

"Me?" The soft look in Nikki's eyes belied the brisk, enough-of-this-nonsense tone of her voice. "You look like you just crawled out of a coal mine." Then, unable to deny herself, she reached up to touch the back of the hand that was smoothing her hair. "Are you sure you're all right?" she asked softly, her voice still unnaturally husky from the smoke. Her gaze searched his face. "You're not burned anywhere?"

"I'm fine," he assured her just as the firemen came racing around the back of the house with the nightshirt-clad Lisbeth in the lead. He lifted his hand to hail them. "We could use some oxygen over here," he said as two of the firemen veered off toward him while the rest of them rushed past, up the terrace steps to the smoke-filled bedroom.

"I don't need any oxygen," Nikki said as she criss-crossed the robe over her torso and pulled the belt tight around her narrow waist. "I'm fine."

"You need oxygen," Pierce said, motioning to one of the firemen to administer it to her whether she wanted it or not.

She sighed and slipped out from under Pierce's sheltering arm as one of the firemen held the oxygen mask to her face.

Pierce stumbled against her as she moved away from him.

Nikki's eyes widened in alarm, vivid green in her soot-smeared face. "I thought you said you weren't hurt," she accused, rudely pushing the oxygen mask out of the way as she reached to steady him. She slipped her arm around his waist before either of the firemen could move to assist him, wedging her shoulder into his armpit to support him.

"Not from the fire," Pierce said, leaning heavily on her as he wrapped his arm around her shoulders again and let her take most of his weight.

"Then what?" Nikki demanded, ignoring the firemen as she steered Pierce to a lounge chair by the pool.

He gave her a lopsided grin, one mingling wry self-deprecation with the sort of pride a fond father feels when his little girl has accomplished a feat he'd thought was beyond her capabilities. "I think you broke my leg when you kicked me."

PIERCE'S LEG WASN'T actually broken. There was a nasty-looking bruise on his shin and X rays revealed a small hairline fracture of the tibia that would need a bit of coddling until it healed. Pierce agreed to having a removable walking cast strapped onto his lower leg by the emergency-room personnel but refused to submit to the indignity of a wheelchair until Nikki grudgingly agreed to lung X rays and an examination for possible injuries caused by smoke inhalation. As this involved the taking of a blood sample to check for possible toxins that may have been present in the smoke, it was awhile before she was finally allowed to return to Pierce's side.

Both Claire and Gage were with him when she entered the examining room that had been set aside for their use. And neither of them, Nikki thought, looked anywhere near as frazzled as they should have at being called out of bed to come to the emergency room in the middle of the night. Even Pierce, still in his soot-smeared sweatpants with a hastily donned black T-shirt and the flexible cast on his leg, looked more as if he were sitting on a movie set discussing the next scene than as if he'd really been injured. It must, Nikki thought, disgruntled, be something in the Kingston genes. No frumpiness allowed.

She smoothed a hand through her hair and pulled the lapels of the brown tweed jacket someone had given her closer together over the front of her borrowed blue silk robe. "Hi," she said softly, a bit hesitant about intruding. They seemed so intent on whatever it was they were discussing.

All three of them turned to look at her.

Pierce smiled as if he'd just been presented with an Academy Award. "Hi, yourself," he said tenderly, and held out his hand. "How're you feeling?"

"Like a pincushion," Nikki said as she came forward in the paper slippers one of the nurses had given her and slipped her hand into his. "I don't know why they had to take blood to check my lungs," she groused.

"Poor baby," he sympathized, and raised her hand to his lips for a brief kiss.

"We were just discussing strategy for dealing with the press," Claire said, one eyebrow raised as she exchanged a meaningful glance with Gage. "They're hovering around outside like a pack of vultures, waiting for the two of you to appear."

"How did they find out so fast?" Nikki asked, appalled. "It's the middle of the night, for God's sake!"

"Actually, it's almost dawn," said Gage. "And they have contacts everywhere. It's their job." He stood up and put his hands on the handles of his brother's wheelchair, prepared to roll it over a few toes if need be. "We might as well get this show on the road," he said grimly. "Ready?"

Claire nodded and took up her position as point man, just ahead of the wheelchair.

Pierce gave Nikki's hand a reassuring squeeze. "Ready," he said.

They moved out of the examining room and through the crowded lobby, their goal the yellow Mercedes station wagon waiting in the red No Parking zone at the curb. The reporters descended on them like hungry fish at feeding time as they exited through the automatic doors of the emergency room. Flashbulbs went off in their faces. Questions came from all sides, fast and thick, and personal. Incredibly personal.

"How long have you and Nikki been lovers?"

"What were you doing when the fire broke out?"

"Were you in bed when the fire started?"

"Were you asleep or . . . ?"

Nikki ducked her head, amazed and exasperated and just a tiny bit frightened by the frenzy, although she would have died before admitting it. Facing the threat of the Iraqi's SCUD missiles had been easier, she thought with a shudder.

"We're almost there," Pierce said bracingly, ignoring from long practice the shouted questions and flash bulbs.

Then, as if they had choreographed the whole thing in advance, Claire veered off to the side and slowed to answer a question, pulling most of the reporters with her just before she reached the car. Pierce came to his feet, reaching out to open the car door as Gage pulled the wheelchair out from under him and swung it around between them and the reporters. At a nudge from Pierce, Nikki slid into the front seat of the Mercedes, scooting over to the middle to give him plenty of room for his leg. Gage slammed the door closed, shutting out the shouted questions, and went around to the driver's side.

"You've done this before," Nikki said admiringly, including both of them in her statement.

"More times than I like to think about," Gage said, reaching for the ignition. The Mercedes purred.

"But what about Claire?" Nikki asked. "Are we going to just leave her there?"

"Don't worry about Claire," Pierce said, glancing at his sister in the side mirror. There was more than a hint of brotherly pride in his voice. "She's a match for any reporter."

Nikki turned her head, leaning over Pierce to look out the window as Gage eased the station wagon away from the curb. "But—" she began.

A flash bulb went off in her face, startling her. "Of all the rude people—" she sputtered, her body tensing as if she meant to crawl over Pierce and go after the reporter.

He put his hand on her leg, calming her. "Ignore them," he said. And then, suddenly weary, he closed his eyes and leaned his head back against the seat. He kept them closed all the way home, rousing again only when Gage turned into the long driveway of the Beverly Hills mansion. His beautiful face looked unnaturally pale, thought Nikki, although that, she mused, might have been in contrast to the streaks of soot still marking his skin. She stared at him, consumed with guilt. If she'd been doing what she'd been hired to do instead of . . . instead of what she'd *been* doing, she thought with a blush, none of this would have happened.

"Are you sure you're all right?" she asked worriedly as they got out of the car in front of the house. "Your leg doesn't hurt too much?"

Pierce managed a weak grin. "It doesn't hurt at all," he assured her in a pained tone intended to let her know how heroically brave he was being.

"Here, lean on me," she said, unconvinced. "I'll help you to your bedr . . ." Her voice trailed off as she realized his bedroom was no longer in any condition to be slept in. "You can sleep in my room," she said contritely, forgetting there were at least a half-a-dozen other bedrooms in the pseudo castle.

Pierce's grin became stronger. "Oh, I intend to," he whispered into her ear as he allowed her to assist him up the wide stone steps and into the house.

His staff converged on them in the front hall, hovering around with suggestions and comments and questions, turning the trip up the wide curving staircase to the second floor into a halting procession. Nikki ignored them all, intent on getting Pierce upstairs. She didn't see Pierce's pirate grin as he waved away his brother's help when Gage came to assist him from the other side. Nor did she notice the black looks cast in her direction from more than one member of Pierce's staff.

Once inside the cozy green-and-ivory bedroom, Nikki left her injured employer to the tender mercies of his brother and the others, hurrying across the room to the open glass doors leading out to the terrace. While she stepped outside to look around and then closed and locked them, Pierce adroitly got rid of his other helpers. He assured Mrs. Gilmore that all he really wanted was a shower and a few hours in the sack, and *then* maybe he could think about breakfast; he instructed Kathy Frye to call Claire about a formal statement for the press; he thanked Lisbeth Greene for her concern.

Doing his best to help, Gage herded everyone out in front of him, pausing in the doorway only long enough to assure his brother that he would take care of calling their parents in Italy "to let them know what really happened before they read about your miraculous escape from death in the morning editions." Then he pulled the door closed behind him as he left.

Pierce leaned back against the closed door and breathed an exaggerated sigh of relief.

"Tired?" Nikki asked, the expression of concern in her eyes softer than she knew as she turned to stare at him from across the width of the room.

Pierce shook his head. "Wired." He held out his hand. "Come here," he ordered softly.

Nikki's expression turned wary. "You told Mrs. Gilmore you wanted to take a shower and then go to sleep," she said, recognizing the look in his eyes from last night.

"I told her I wanted to take a shower and then go to bed," he corrected her with a hint of his pirate's smile.

"There's a difference." He wriggled his fingers at her in a beckoning motion. "Come here, sweetheart."

Nikki hesitated, her hands clutching the door handle behind her, torn between what she wanted to do and what she knew she should do. It was just this sort of thing that had caused her dereliction of duty in the first place. "Your leg . . ." she whispered, trying to remind herself of all the reasons why she shouldn't.

"Damn my leg," Pierce said irritably. And then he smiled again, abruptly deciding a change of tactics was in order. "My leg is fine. See?" he said, pushing away from the door to show her. He stumbled a bit. "Well, maybe not so fine," he admitted, looking at her from under his lashes to see how she was taking it. After a moment's hesitation—during which he managed to take two limping half steps—she reacted exactly the way he hoped she would.

"Don't put any more weight on the leg than you have to," she said, hurrying across the carpet to help him. "Just take it slow and easy. That's it," she crooned, trying to ignore the way her pulse had begun to race the moment he put his arm around her shoulders. "We'll just get you into the bathroom." She maneuvered him in that direction with one arm around his waist and the other hand flat against his chest for balance. "And then I'll run down and see if I can catch Gage before he leaves." She moved to slip out from under his arm.

He tightened his grip around her shoulders, shifting it a bit so that she was standing more in front of him than at his side. "Gage?" he murmured, giving in to the urge to nuzzle her ear.

She pushed against his chest with the flat of her hand, keeping as much room between her body and his as possible. "To help you undress and take a shower," she said briskly, trying to pretend her heart wasn't attempting to pound its way out of her chest at the mere thought of him naked and wet.

"I'd rather have you help me."

I'd rather have me help you, too, she thought. "I don't think that's a good idea," she said instead, staring at her hand on his chest as she spoke.

"Why not?"

She risked a quick glance at his face. "You know very well why not."

"Because you think one of us is going to get turned on if you do?"

Because one of us already is, she thought.

"I have a news flash for you, sweetheart," he said, his voice warm with tender amusement. "One of us already is."

That brought her head up. "How did you—"

"I'm so turned on I can hardly stand up but—" he gave a little shrug, disarming and artless "—there's not a lot I can do about it right now."

Unable to stop herself, Nikki glanced down at the front of his sweatpants. Her expression, when her gaze flickered briefly back to his, was patently disbelieving.

Pierce smiled. "Despite all evidence to the contrary," he said, his voice solemn in spite of the look in his eyes—and the condition of his body, "I *am* temporarily disabled." *For chasing you down, anyway,* he thought, although he would if he had to. He wanted her badly enough to do just about anything. "And even if I wasn't, I fail to see the problem." He locked his hands at the small of her back, loosely, and touched his forehead to hers. "And it isn't as if you haven't seen all there is to see."

"Well, yes, I know, but . . ." But it had been dark last night and she hadn't really seen anything at all and neither had he and . . .

"I'd really like to wash off all this sweat and soot," he murmured cajolingly. "It itches." His breath was warm on her skin, as tantalizing as a kiss. "It must be making you itch, too."

"Well, yes, but . . ."

He nuzzled her with his nose, tickling her with the butterfly brush of his eyelashes. "Take a shower with me, Nikki."

She felt her spine begin to dissolve. "I don't think . . ." she began, and then forgot what it was she intended to say.

"I promise not to take advantage of the situation," he murmured, his lips just millimeters away from hers. "I won't even look if you don't want me to."

"Promise?" The breathy word was a heated puff of air against his mouth, rife with her desire to surrender.

He crossed his fingers behind her back. "Promise."

"All right." She sighed and tilted her head for his kiss.

He dropped his arms and drew back without giving it to her, smiling to himself at the look of disappointment that crossed her face. There were a hundred different strategies to the game of love and he knew them all. Teaching them to the reluctantly passionate Ms. Martinelli was going to be a distinct and thoroughly unique pleasure.

"I like the water hot," he said casually, reaching up behind his head with one hand to grab the neck of his T-shirt. He pulled it off, dropping it onto the floor, and sat down on the lid of the toilet seat to untie his shoes and remove the cast. "I hope that's all right with you."

"It's fine," Nikki said faintly, watching him yank at the laces of his shoes and the Velcro fastenings of the cast, wondering if she'd read him wrong, after all. Maybe he did only want her to help him take a shower before he went to sleep. He *had* dozed off in the car. And a hairline fracture was probably enough to cause a mild case of shock in even the strongest man. Not to mention the trauma of the fire. Maybe she was just projecting her own desires onto him and he didn't want . . .

And then he stood up, tugging at the drawstring on his sweat-pants so that they fell down around his ankles, and she didn't have any doubts at all about his desires. He was fully, magnificently erect. Pulsating with arousal.

Unconsciously Nikki licked her lips. Her pupils dilated to nearly twice their normal size, nearly obscuring the pale green of her irises.

Pierce caught the heated look in her eyes and almost lost it right there. He made himself look away, struggling to retain the thin hold he had on his control. "Are you planning to take a shower in your clothes?" he asked, stepping out of the pool of fabric around his ankles with credible calm, wondering if playing games had been such a good idea, after all.

I should get a frigging Academy Award for this performance, he thought as he limped to the oversized shower stall and reached inside to turn on the taps. Water sprayed out of two shower heads. He held his hand beneath the juncture of the twin streams, waiting for it to warm, thinking that he should probably step into it now, while it was still cold enough to do some good, instead of standing there, listening intently for the whispers of sound that would tell him she was finally undressing.

When they didn't come, he turned his head, glancing over his shoulder to see what the problem was. She was still standing there, staring at him with that fascinated look on her face, as if she were utterly absorbed by him. It humbled him and made him proud, all at the same time. "Do you want me to help you?" he asked softly, awed by that look. In all his life, no woman had ever looked at him in just exactly that way.

"No," she said. "No, I can do it."

He nodded, waiting.

Shyly, then, realizing he wasn't going to turn away again, suddenly not wanting him to, she toed off the paper slippers and lifted her hands to the front of the borrowed jacket, pushing it off her shoulders. It fell to the floor, sliding down the backs of her legs as she reached for the sash of the blue silk robe. Slowly, watching his face for the slightest hint of a reaction, she pulled it loose.

The robe parted, revealing a tantalizing slice of her slender body—the inside curves of her small breasts, her narrow rib cage, her flat belly with its tiny dent of a naval, the thatch of silky black hair between her thighs.

Pierce stood very still, waiting and watching, his eyes as hot as laser beams while moist clouds of steam filled the small tiled room.

Nikki steeled herself and took that final step, giving her fragile woman's pride fully into his keeping, trusting that he would find her long, gangly, soot-streaked body as beautiful as she found his. She shrugged her shoulders, sending the robe sliding down her back to the floor, and waited for his verdict.

His eyes widened, darkening nearly to navy as he took his first fully unobstructed look at her. His chest swelled with a long indrawn breath. His hand clenched painfully around the edge of the shower door. His erection twitched, alive and straining toward her. He moved his lips, soundlessly forming her name, and held out his hand.

She smiled tremulously, her relief evident in her eyes, and put her hand in his.

He drew her toward him slowly, stepping backward into the shower as she moved forward, reaching around her to pull the door closed behind her. Their bodies touched, lightly at first, and then they were in each other's arms, plastered together under the warm spray of the shower. Their lips met in a searing open-mouthed kiss, desperate to take and taste, reckless with intemperate need, rife with unrestrained passion. It lasted forever and still wasn't long enough to even begin to satisfy their hunger for each other.

"You nearly drove me crazy, woman," Pierce said, dragging his mouth away from hers to press it against her cheeks and jaw and the fragile lids of her eyes. "I thought I was going to have to tear those clothes off you."

"Would you have?" she asked in a throaty whisper, thrilled that he wanted her that much.

"In two seconds flat," he vowed. He took her head in his hands, smoothing her wet hair back from her forehead and temples, his thumbs rubbing lightly at the smears of soot that lingered on her elegant cheekbones, his gaze hot and devouring as it roamed over her upturned face. "God, you're beautiful," he said, and kissed her again. "Every long, slinky, sexy inch of you. Soot and all."

She smiled then, a slow smile, full of newly discovered feminine power. "You said you wouldn't take advantage of the situation," she reminded him teasingly, rubbing her hard little nipples against his chest as she said it.

He grinned his pirate's grin. "I had my fingers crossed." He backed her up against the tile wall of the shower and pressed his hardened body into the softness of hers, letting her feel his desire. "I intend to take full and complete advantage of you *and* the situation," he added, sliding his hands down to cup her breasts, "every blessed chance I get."

She arched against his touch, pressing her breasts into his palms. "Is that another one of your flimsy promises?"

"Solid gold," he whispered, dragging his mouth down the long column of her throat. "You can take it to the bank."

"I'd rather you just—" she gasped as his mouth closed over the engorged tip of her breast "—take me," she said with a breathless sigh. Her fingers dug into his shoulders. "*Now,*" she demanded fiercely.

He groaned and bent his knees, sliding his hands to her thighs to lift her for his entry. The groan turned to a strangled sound of pain and frustration as his injured leg protested the move. "Damn it to hell!" The words were grated out through clenched teeth. "It isn't going to work this way."

His leg wasn't going to hold up under their combined weight or the force of the thrusts his enflamed body was urging him to make. And, he realized as the stab of pain cleared his senses, that wasn't the only problem: he'd been about to take her without protection. He started to pull away, his mind sorting through all the ways there were to solve both dilemmas.

Nikki clutched him tighter, too far gone to understand what he'd said, knowing only that he was pulling away just at the moment when she needed him most desperately. "Pierce?" she said with a low, aching moan.

"It's all right, sweetheart." He slid his hand from the back of her thigh to the slippery softness between her legs and thrust two long fingers into the swollen depths of her, knowing what would assuage her need.

She arched against him. "More," she urged, and thrust her hips against his hand.

He gave her more and then more, until he felt the rhythmic convulsions of her body around his fingers, but it still wasn't enough to satisfy her. "More," she said again, her slender body straining against him as if she hadn't just achieved climax. She reached down, pressing her fingers into his tight buttocks, pulling his hips against hers, tilting her pelvis in ancient, unmistakable invitation and entreaty. "More," she demanded, and bit him on the shoulder.

Pierce groaned. "Nikki, sweetheart...please," he said raggedly, driven to the very limits of his control by her passionate demand. "I'm trying to be sensible here." He groaned again as she slid her hand between their bodies and curled her fingers around him.

"I want you inside me, Pierce," she said, squeezing him. "I *need* you inside me."

Pierce's control broke. He pushed away from the shower wall with one hand, pulling her along with an arm around her waist as he slid her feet backward over the floor of the shower. The backs of his legs touched the low tile bench against the opposite wall and he sat down, pulling her onto his lap with her thighs astride his as he did so. He put his hands on her hips, holding her still when she would have sunk down onto the turgid length of him. "I haven't got any condoms," he said, feeling compelled to make sure she knew that. "Nikki, look at me," he demanded raggedly, forcing himself to wait until she did so.

She lifted heavy-lidded, passion-glazed eyes to his.

"You won't be protected if we do this now."

"I don't want to be protected." She cupped his face in her hands. "I only want you," she said, and leaned forward to touch her lips to his. "Make love to me, Pierce," she whispered achingly against his mouth.

All of Pierce's noble intentions fled in the face of her passionate entreaty. One hand moved down to guide his iron-hard tumescence into the heated core of her. The other hand moved to cup the back of her head. "Kiss me," he demanded hoarsely, thrusting his tongue into her mouth as he thrust his eager, aching manhood into her welcoming body.

The effect was instantaneous and intense. They exploded together in a blaze of white-hot heat that went on and on, holding them at the very pinnacle of physical sensation. They held tight to each other, their bodies straining, their emotions soaring, and rode it out.

Exquisite, Pierce thought, when he could think again. It was the most exquisite sensation he'd ever experienced. So hot and sweet it almost hurt, and more perfect than anything had ever been before. He wondered, vaguely, as he sat there holding her trembling body in his arms, if the intensity of the experience had something to do with the way they'd tempted fate, with the knowledge that now, this very minute, one of his sperm could be wriggling its way into one of her eggs, creating a whole new life. Just the possibility of it made him feel—he sifted around in his mind for just the right word—primitive, he decided. It made him feel primitive. Basic. Primordial.

He was getting hard again, just thinking about it.

"What?" Nikki murmured, her breath warm against his neck.

"More," Pierce groaned raggedly, and put his hands on her hips to show her the movement that would bring them both to exquisite pleasure once again.

9

ALL OF THE KINGSTON siblings were present much later that afternoon for what Pierce factitiously termed "a little alfresco luncheon" and Nikki privately thought of as a strategic gathering of the clan. The meal was served out under one of the umbrella tables by the swimming pool. The chicken salad in pineapple shells, the date-nut bread and cinnamon-spiced iced tea were accompanied by the acrid smell of stale smoke and charred wool carpeting and the sounds of the cleanup crew hard at work in the room upstairs.

The fire itself had done very little damage. It had smoldered for a good while before it finally burst into flame so, aside from the carpet, the damage was mostly cosmetic. Painters, carpet layers and the same interior decorator who had been employed when Pierce first purchased the house were already scheduled to begin their work once the cleanup was complete. The insurance investigator had already been and gone. An art restoration expert had been called in to deal with the smoke damage done to the paintings that had been hanging in the bedroom, as well as to inspect the pieces in the upstairs hall. And a call had been put in to various clothing stores, including the very trendy Maxfield, to replenish Pierce's wardrobe, which had also suffered from the smoke that had drifted into every crack and cranny of his bedroom. By the end of the week, when the smell of fresh paint and new carpeting had eradicated the smell of smoke, no one would be able to tell there had ever been a fire.

"There's not really much damage, considering," Gage commented idly, watching his superstar brother feed the baby sitting in the high chair between them.

Pierce glanced down at the removable walking cast strapped to his lower left leg. "Not to the bedroom, anyway," he said dryly.

Gage grinned at him. "Given the fact that you were kicked by a battle-seasoned marine trained in—what is it you're trained in?" he asked Nikki.

"Dirty street fighting," Pierce said, turning his head to smile at the woman sitting beside him. The baby smacked the high chair tray with both hands, conveying his displeasure at the interruption in the delivery of his meal. "Okay, okay, hold your diaper on," Pierce said, and quickly inserted another spoonful of strained peaches into his nephew's wide-open mouth. "If she'd fought fair," he said to his brother, "I could've taken her."

"You wish," Gage snorted, and winked at Nikki.

She smiled back.

"Oh, good Lord, will you look at what's in the *Star,*" Tara exclaimed in dismay, snapping the paper between her hands as she folded it open.

"Wait, don't tell me, let me guess," Pierce said his tone half amused, half disgusted. There was a stack of tabloids on the table and each one of them told a story more fantastic than the one before. "The fire was set by my supposed new wife—" he inclined his head toward Nikki "—in a fit of jealousy because I refuse to give up all my old lovers and cleave only unto her. No, wait," he said, adroitly scooping strained peaches off his nephew's chin with the tip of a baby-sized spoon as he spoke, "it was started by my alien lover from the planet Krypton because she's jealous of Nikki."

"Pierce, please," Claire said, setting aside the paper she'd been skimming to take the one her sister-in-law held out to her. "Oh, my," she said after a quick glance at the headline. "It's not about the fire at all." She cast a wry look at her brother over the edge of the paper. "Not the one you're referring to, anyway."

Something in her tone warned Pierce that he wasn't going to like whatever it was. "What then?" he asked, instinctively glancing at the dark-haired woman seated next to him. She probably wasn't going to like it, either.

"Well, the good news is, they seem to have swallowed the ruse of your make-believe af—that is," she amended hastily, tactfully avoiding mentioning that the affair no longer seemed to be make-believe, "they haven't ferreted out the fact that Nikki's your bodyguard, so your macho reputation is still intact."

"And the bad news?" Pierce prompted.

Claire hesitated, exchanging a concerned glance with Tara over Nikki's possible reaction to having her private life suddenly becoming very public. It was bad enough when you were accustomed to seeing the events of your life misrepresented in print; it had to be pure hell when you weren't.

"Claire?" Pierce prodded, a forgotten spoonful of strained peaches held in midair as he waited for her answer.

The baby screwed up his face.

Gage reached over and plucked the spoon out of his brother's fingers, averting a noisy outburst by quickly and efficiently slipping the contents into his son's mouth without spilling a drop.

"Go ahead and read it aloud," Nikki said with a sigh, correctly interpreting the worried glances that passed between the other two women. "We might as well know the worst."

"There's a picture of the two of you, um...dancing." Claire said delicately. She folded the paper in half and reached across the table, laying it between Pierce and Nikki's plates.

Gage lifted an eyebrow. "New step?" he asked facetiously, trying to lighten the suddenly tense mood.

Tara shook her head at her husband, warning him that now was not the time to tease his brother, no matter how pure his motive. Nikki made a strangled noise and covered her eyes with her hand.

Pierce frowned and reached out to pick up the paper.

The photographer had captured them mid-kiss on the dance floor. Their bodies were pressed together, as close as two panting teenagers in the back seat of a car. Their arms were wrapped around each other as if they never intended to let go. Their tongues were very obviously down each other's throats. It was hot and passionate and carnal and...

And private, damn it, Pierce thought, his hand fisting on the newspaper as he skimmed the accompanying text. His upper lip curled. "That's it!" he snarled, tossing the tabloid down in the middle of the table. "This time they've gone too far. I want you to call the lawyers on this one, Claire," he ordered.

"Lawyers?" Gage asked as he exchanged a significant look with his wife and sister. Pierce had never threatened legal action over a news story before, no matter how outrageous. Usually, the more outrageous the story, the more it amused him.

"That article is a blatant invasion of privacy," Pierce fumed.

"A dance floor is hardly what I'd call private," Claire began dryly, only to be silenced by a look from Gage.

"At least they spelled your name right," he said, watching Pierce carefully as he paraphrased the old Hollywood maxim that said any publicity was good publicity as long as they spelled your name right. It was a platitude Pierce had repeated more than once himself, usually when some other member of the family was fuming over some scandalous bit of tabloid gossip. "And it will all blow over in a week or two, anyway, so what's the fuss?" Gage continued. That, too, was something Pierce had been heard to say.

Pierce looked at his brother as if he'd lost his mind. "And in the meantime, the whole damn world is speculating about my—" he looked at Nikki "—about *our* private life."

Gage grinned. "It's never bothered you before."

Pierce just glared at him.

"I don't understand," Nikki said then, staring at him as if he were the one who'd lost his mind. "Publicity was the whole point, wasn't it? It was the reason we went out last night and why you kissed me and . . . everything," she said euphemistically, coloring slightly as she remembered that his whole family was listening to their exchange. "So everyone would think we were—" she shrugged "—involved."

Pierce stopped her with a look. "I thought we settled that last night," he said sternly. "I did not kiss you to make anyone think anything. I kissed you and . . . everything," he imitated her hesitation perfectly, "because I wanted to. Desperately," he added, not the least bit embarrassed by the presence of his family. "Is that absolutely clear?"

"But you can't deny that that's why we went out in the first pl—"

He reached out and caught her chin between his thumb and forefinger. "Is that clear?"

Nikki stared into his eyes for a long moment. "Clear," she said softly, warmed by the look in his eyes. "You kissed me because you wanted to."

"Don't forget it," Pierce ordered, and leaned forward in his chair to kiss her again—hard and emphatically—before he let her go.

"But you still can't deny we went out in the first place to stir up just this kind of speculation," she said when he released her. "The whole idea was to draw out the writer of the fan letters."

Pierce sighed. "And we drew out every scandalmonger in Hollywood instead."

"Not necessarily," Nikki said slowly as an idea that had been fermenting in the back of her mind pushed its way to the front. "Maybe we did both."

"The fire was an accident, pure and simple," Pierce said, knowing where she was going before she got there. "You heard the firemen last night. A log rolled out of the fireplace."

Nikki shot him a challenging look. "And what if it didn't?"

Pierce shook his head. "That's crazy."

"No, it's not crazy," Nikki insisted, her conviction growing stronger in the face of his knee-jerk opposition. "It's not crazy at all. Think about it for a minute. How easy would it be for a log to roll out of that fireplace? The andirons are huge. And you put the screen back in place after you lit the fire last night. I remember watching you do it."

"So what are you saying?" Pierce asked. "That this mysterious letter writer tiptoed into the bedroom in the middle of the night and deliberately started the fire by dragging a log out of the fireplace?"

"It's possible."

"It's ridiculous," Pierce scoffed.

"Why is it ridiculous?" Nikki wanted to know. "Because you want it to be?" She shook her head. "Whoever wrote those letters said she couldn't stand the thought of another betrayal," she said, reminding them all of the threat implicit in the wording of the last letter. "She said she'd do anything she had to to prevent it, even if it meant losing you."

"Are you listening to yourself?" Pierce asked. "Do you hear what you're suggesting?"

"She's suggesting that some jealous, and quite possibly insane, fan tried to make good on her threat last night," Claire said tartly. "She's suggesting that someone might have tried to kill you."

"By setting fire to a room I wasn't even in?"

"It was dark," Nikki reminded him. "Even with the fire in the fireplace, all anyone would have seen was a lump under the covers. It was your room," she pointed out. "The logical assumption would have been that it was you in the bed."

"Oh, jeez." Pierce yanked his napkin off his lap and threw it onto the table with enough force to make the silverware jump. "I don't believe this."

Little Beau jerked in surprise, startled by his uncle's action, and began to cry.

"It's okay, son," Gage said, reaching to lift the baby out of his high chair. "Nobody's yelling at you."

Tara stood up and pushed her chair back. "Give him to me," she said, holding out her arms for her baby. "I'll take him inside and get him cleaned up. It's okay, Beau," she crooned gently, cuddling the baby to her. "Uncle Pierce didn't mean to scare you . . . did you, Uncle Pierce?"

"Hell, no, kid," Pierce said contritely, smiling broadly as he reached up to tickle the baby under his peach-smeared chin. "I was trying to scare some sense into someone else entirely."

Beau chuckled in delight and blew a bubbly raspberry.

"That means you're forgiven," Tara interpreted with a smile. "Come on, sweetie." She patted the baby's diapered bottom. "Let's go get you changed."

"Nikki's right, you know," Gage said after Tara and Beau had disappeared inside the house. "Someone might very well have tried to kill you last night. Or, at the very least, been issuing a strong warning."

"Warning?"

"She did say she'd do anything she had to do to stop you from betraying her again."

"Well, there you go," Pierce said, thinking he'd just had his point made for him. "Whoever she is, she couldn't have known about my so-called betrayal last night—" he motioned toward the stack of tabloids on the table "—because it wasn't public knowledge until today."

"She could have seen us at Spago," Nikki said. "Or the club. She could have . . ." She bit her lower lip, hesitating to say it out loud because of how he'd reacted the last time she'd suggested the culprit might be someone he knew.

"She could have what?" Gage demanded quietly, his amber eyes watchful as he looked back and forth between the stern, set faces of his brother and his brother's bodyguard.

"She could have seen us here, after we got back," Nikki said, still staring intently at Pierce. "Or she could have been here all along. Waiting."

There was a long tense silence as her listeners digested her statement.

"I never thought of that," Claire said finally.

"Because the idea is completely ludicrous," Pierce said. "That's why you never thought of it."

"No," Claire said thoughtfully. "No, I think it's because I've been too close to the situation." She looked at both of her brothers in turn. "We've all been too close to the situation. But Nikki could be right. It could be—"

"Oh, come on, Claire. It could be Lisbeth, is that what you're saying? It could be Kathy? Or how about Mrs. Gilmore? Or the gardener?"

Claire frowned. "When you put it that way, it does sound ridiculous, but damn it all—" she struck her fist lightly on the table "—it still makes a strange kind of sense."

"In what way?"

"As I said before, whoever wrote those letters knows an awful lot about your movements. More," she said, anticipating his objections, "than anyone would know just by reading the tabloids. That's bothered me from the beginning. And yet, to let myself even consider the possibility that it might be someone we know... someone who might even live here..." She shook her head. "I don't know what to think."

"It doesn't have to be someone who actually lives here," Nikki said. "It could be someone who has access. Like the gardener. I've seen her watching Pierce when she thinks nobody's looking," she explained, answering their unasked questions. "She stares at him as if he were some kind of god."

"Oh, jeez . . ."

"Yes, I've noticed, too," Claire said thoughtfully. "I hadn't thought anything of it before, but—"

"Because there's nothing *to* think of it," Pierce said.

"And she's here—what?—once or twice a week?" Claire went on, ignoring her brother's outburst. "She has access to the whole house, too."

"There are lots of other people who have access to the house," Nikki reminded them. "Or to the grounds, at least. Pool maintenance, deliveries, the cleaning service people who come in to help Mrs. Gilmore." She shrugged. "Any number of people, really. As far as I can tell, the gates out front are never closed, let alone locked. And they should be. Especially now."

"Yes," Claire agreed, with a sidelong glance at her brother to see how he was taking it. "They should be."

He wasn't taking it well. "Damn it, Claire," he said. "I've never let strangers influence how I live my life and I'm not about to start now. I refuse to live in some kind of armed camp with barricades and alarms and—"

"Excuse me," Kathy Frye said. "I don't like to interrupt a family lunch, but I thought you'd want to see this right away."

Pierce looked up at his secretary with a smile. Everyone else looked away guiltily, afraid Kathy would see that they'd considered her among their list of suspects. "What is it?" Pierce asked.

"The mail came a few minutes ago. This was with it." She laid an envelope beside Pierce's plate. It was plain white, like that which could be found in any stationery store, addressed to Mr. Pierce Kingston in aqua ink. There was a "love" stamp in the corner but it hadn't, Nikki noticed, been canceled by the post office. It could have been an oversight—such things did occasionally happen—or it could mean that the letter had been placed in the mailbox by someone other than the mail carrier.

"I opened it before I realized what it was," Kathy said, explaining the condition of the envelope. "I hope I didn't destroy any clues or anything."

"That's fine, Kathy," Claire said, her tone politely but quite clearly dismissing the secretary. "Thank you."

Kathy glanced at Pierce, her expression questioning, but he was staring at the letter lying beside his plate. She nodded at Claire and went back in the house.

"Do you want me to read it?" Claire asked when Pierce continued to stare at the letter.

He shook his head and picked the envelope up, carefully, as if it might bite him. Slipping two fingers into the open slit, he extracted the single sheet of lined pastel blue paper inside and unfolded it. There was only one sentence on the paper.

"*I warned you about the other women,*" Pierce read aloud.

10

NIKKI SAT SILENTLY, staring into the snifter of Armagnac between her hands as if the words she needed were hidden somewhere in the golden depths of the fifty-year-old brandy. She'd been trying to think of a way to say what had to be said ever since the fan letter had been delivered at lunch. Trying, too, to find the proper time and place to say it.

The house had been full of people all day: Pierce's family and staff; the insurance investigators; the cleanup crew; salesclerks from the most ritzy men's stores on Rodeo Drive, salivating at the chance to completely replenish Pierce Kingston's wardrobe; an interior decorator who kept trying to get Pierce to look at wallpaper books and fabric samples when he'd already made it clear he wanted his bedroom restored to exactly what it had been before the fire; reporters showing up unannounced, trying to wheedle an interview with anyone who would talk to them. Now—except for Mrs. Gilmore, who'd disappeared into her suite of rooms off the kitchen as soon as dinner had been cleared away—they were alone.

It was just coming on dusk. The faint glow of sunset still colored the sky, sending slanting rays of rose-colored light through the windows of the garden room. In a few minutes it would be full dark. There was music playing in the background, something soft and soothing that Nikki thought she recognized. The faint scent of sandalwood potpourri gently scented the air. It was all so romantic.

Nikki sighed.

"Tired?" Pierce said, sitting down on the sofa beside her. He lifted his bare feet to the glass-and-cypress coffee table, crossing them at the ankles, and leaned back against the plump chintz cushions with a heartfelt sigh of his own. "Personally, I'm beat," he said, inhaling the fumes of the Armagnac in his glass before taking a sip. "It's been way too hectic around here today to suit me." He stretched one arm out along the sofa back behind Nikki's head and, very lightly, stroked the hair behind her ear with one long finger. "I'm glad everyone's gone."

Nikki looked up with a quick, nervous smile, like a tongue-tied schoolgirl too shy to say anything, and then ducked her head to take a tiny sip of her drink. *Now*, she told herself. *Right now, before he finishes his drink and decides to take up where we left off this morning in the shower.*

"Penny for your thoughts?" Pierce said.

Nikki took a breath and told herself to simply say it. "I was just wondering what the name of that song is," she said, without looking at him. "It sounds familiar."

"That particular piece is by Debussy. *Claire de Lune.*"

Nikki nodded her head as if his answer had meant something to her. "It's nice."

"Yes," Pierce said, staring at her averted face. "It is." He ran his finger down the curve of her cheek. "Why don't you try telling me what's really on your mind?"

Nikki continued to stare into the snifter between her hands. "We have to talk."

"About what?"

"About . . ." Why was it so hard to say? "About us."

"What about us?" he asked carefully, sensing danger.

Nikki took another sip of her drink, a larger one this time, and set the snifter on the coffee table in front of her. "We can't continue like this."

"Could you be a bit more specific?"

"Like this." She waved her hand back and forth between them. "The way we are . . . here . . . now."

"Does that mean you just want to go straight up to the bedroom and forget the foreplay?" Pierce asked, trying for a little humor.

Nikki lifted her head then, and just looked at him. "You know what I mean."

Pierce sighed. "Yes," he said. "I'm afraid I do." He lifted his snifter to his lips, draining it in one long swallow, and then leaned forward to set it onto the glass-topped table next to Nikki's. "Do you mind telling me why?" he asked, trying very hard to stay calm.

"Because it shouldn't have happened in the first place, that's why," Nikki said. "Because I work for you. Because I can't do my job when I'm distracted by . . ."

"Sex?" Pierce supplied when she hesitated.

"Yes," Nikki said, trying not to blush. That wasn't what she'd been going to say—she wasn't quite sure of the word she would have used—but it would do. "And last night proved it. If I hadn't let myself get . . . distracted, I might have been able to prevent what happened. I might even have been able to catch whoever did it, *before* she did it."

"I could fire you," Pierce suggested.

"What?"

"I could fire you and ask Bender to send over another bodyguard," Pierce said, only half kidding.

"Then you wouldn't have to worry about being distracted."

Nikki stared at him, her expression both incredulous and indignant.

Pierce suddenly had the feeling he'd gone a step too far. "It's a solution to our problem," he said, with a halfhearted attempt at a casual shrug.

"It's a solution to *your* problem, you mean." Nikki surged to her feet, incensed by his lack of sensitivity. "If you try to fire me because I won't sleep with you, I'll slap you with a sexual harassment suit so fast your head will spin. And just think what that would do to your precious reputation when the tabloids got a hold of it."

"Jeez, Nikki," Pierce said, utterly amazed by the intensity of her outburst. He got to his feet, too, putting out a hand to touch her. "Calm down."

She lifted her chin and took a deliberate step back, out of his reach.

He dropped his hand to his side. "Look, I'm sorry. It was just a joke."

"A very poor joke."

"All right, yes," he agreed. "A very poor joke. And I'm sorry for making it. Okay?"

She glared at him for a moment longer. "Okay," she said finally, grudgingly.

"You want to sit back down now? I'll get us another drink and we can start this discussion over."

Nikki sat. "I don't want another drink," she said.

"Well, I sure as hell do." He went to the bar and poured himself a healthy drink and then came back and sat down next to her, keeping a little more distance between them than he had before. "Okay, talk," he said, calmer now.

"I've given this a lot of thought," Nikki began, "and I just don't feel we can continue what we started last night."

"Why not?"

"Because I can't be your bodyguard and your . . . your . . ."

"My lover," Pierce suggested.

"Yes, all right. I can't be your bodyguard and your lover, too. What happened last night should be proof enough of that."

"Do you really think that if you hadn't been sleeping in my bed you might have stopped whoever it was from starting that fire?"

"I might have. But we'll never know, will we? Because I *was* in your bed. And I was there again this morning, too. If I'd been up and awake, doing my job like I'm supposed to, I might have seen who put that letter in the mailbox. As it is—" She shrugged.

"Do you really think you can end what's between us just like that?" He lifted his hand and gently caressed her cheek, touched by her sweet naiveté. "Do you think you can make all that passion and heat inside you disappear just by willing it to go away?"

"Maybe not," she said, and stood up, unable to bear his touch without wanting to feel his arms close around her. "But I can ignore it. And if I can't—" she looked at him from across the width of the coffee table "—then you won't have to fire me, because I'll quit."

"I don't want you to do that."

"I don't want to do it, either, but I will if I have to. Walking away from a job before it's finished wouldn't hurt nearly as much as getting you killed because I didn't have my mind on what I was doing."

Pierce stared at her for a long, silent moment, awed all over again. She really was like the Amazon goddess he'd first compared her to, he thought, one of that legendary breed of fierce and honorable warrior-women. He had no doubt at all that she meant exactly what she said. She'd walk away rather than compromise her principles. And he'd lose her, right then and there, if he forced her to alter her vision of herself.

His decision made, Pierce stood up. "All right," he said, and held out his hand. "From now on it will be strictly business. Deal?"

Nikki put her hand in his. "Deal," she said, her relief evident in her voice.

And the minute this is over, Pierce promised himself, *all deals are off.* He'd have his Amazon on her back so fast she'd think she'd been tackled by the entire defensive line of the reigning Super Bowl team.

"IT'S A VERY BASIC SYSTEM. Extremely simple to operate," Nikki said the next afternoon, explaining the security system she'd had installed in the front gates. "The mechanism works off a transmitter, like an automatic garage door opener, so you don't even have to get out of the car to open and close the gates. And they can be operated from the house at this panel." She indicated the shiny new wall-mounted panel next to the kitchen telephone. "This button opens and closes the gate. The button below it activates the intercom. Press it down to speak. Release it to listen. The camera—" she flicked a hand at the video screen that made up the left side of the panel "—will be on all the time, monitoring everyone who goes in or out. And I'll make sure there's always enough tape in the recorder, so you don't have to worry about operating that."

"And how will I know someone's at the gate?" asked Mrs. Gilmore, a touch of asperity in her voice. "I can't be looking out all the time to see."

"You won't have to," Nikki informed her. "There's a bell, just like when someone is at the front door." She glanced around the kitchen, her eyes touching each one of them—Pierce, Kathy Frye and Mrs. Gilmore—in turn. "Starting today, I don't want anyone to open the gates without first knowing who's on the other side. If someone says he's delivering groceries or flowers or whatever and you don't recognize him—or her," she said significantly, "I want you to ask for a picture ID. Have them hold it up to the camera so you can get a good look at it. I know it will seem like a lot of bother at first, but pretty soon it will be second nature. And it's important." She turned back to the panel. "Now, this—" she indicated the red button at the bottom of the panel "—is the panic button. It's connected directly to Bender Security. If you press this button and don't call Bender Security within two minutes—the number's right there on the bulletin board—they alert the police and fire departments and the paramedics, plus dispatching security personnel of their own. Four other panic buttons have been installed in the house. By the front door—where there's also another intercom and monitor—in Mr. Kingston's bedroom, in the garden room and in the cabana. Any questions?"

Pierce clicked his heels together and gave her a snappy salute.

"Dogs?" Pierce said. "You really think we need dogs patrolling the grounds?"

"Unless you want me to tell Bill to go ahead and send a crew in to wire the wall," Nikki said, already knowing he didn't, because they'd discussed it. Loudly and at length. She wondered if their new tendency to argue with each other at the drop of a hat had anything to do with their sublimation of other, more basic, tendencies. She suspected it did. "I could have him install the motion-detection system in the house while he's at it," she added provocatively.

"No. Definitely not." Pierce's tone brooked no argument on that score. "I don't want my home run like some armed camp with everyone having to punch in some code every time they want to go in or out of the house. *I* don't want to have to punch a code."

"It could be set up so that it's only activated at night, after everyone's gone to bed, and turned off in the morning. That wouldn't inconvenience anyone. Much."

"And what if I wake up in the middle of the night and feel like doing a few laps or going to the cabana to work out? What if I just want to sit outside on the terrace and drink myself into a stupor?" he said. "What if Mrs. Gilmore can't sleep and gets up to make herself a cup of hot milk?"

"It would only be for a little while, until this woman is caught."

Pierce shook his head. "A security system like that is expensive to install, which means it's ex—"

"At twelve million a picture," Nikki said dryly, "I think you can afford it."

"Which means," he repeated, trying to quell her with a look, "that it's expensive to rip out. And that expense is seen as wasteful, especially by people like you. And Claire. So it becomes a permanent fixture. I don't want it."

"Then it'll have to be the dogs."

Pierce snorted to show his displeasure. "Which means, I assume, that I can look forward to having my throat ripped out by some slobbering Doberman one night on my way to the cabana?"

"Dobermans don't slobber," Nikki informed him tartly. "They're very neat, elegant dogs. Nothing like their publicity would lead you to believe." She flashed him a taunting grin. "A fact which I'm sure you can appreciate. But that's a moot point, because Bill doesn't use Dobermans."

"Why not?" Pierce growled irritably, intrigued in spite of himself. "I thought Dobermans were the world's greatest guard dogs."

"They're too easily disabled."

"By who? Schwarzenegger?"

"No, really, I'm serious," Nikki said. "If you can keep your head and not panic, just about any average adult can fend off a Doberman. Their long legs and necks make them very fragile. Besides that, the breed as a whole is too smart for security work. It makes them undependable."

Pierce lifted an eyebrow.

"If a Doberman's been hurt in the line of duty, he's apt to refuse to participate the next time the same situation comes up."

"So what does Bender use, then? Pit bulls?"

"Same thing the military uses. German shepherds. A German shepherd is all heart. It'll take a bullet and—what?" she said, catching the look in his eye.

"You're just so damn cute when you get all macho and military," Pierce said.

Nikki threw a book at him.

"I REALLY DON'T LIKE all this prying into people's private lives," Pierce said as Nikki slid her finger under the flap of a large manilla envelope. It had been delivered by messenger from Bender Security and placed directly into her hands.

"Think of it as an in-depth reference check," Nikki said as she extracted the contents of the envelope. "You do check references when you hire someone, don't you?"

"Claire does them," Pierce said. "She's my business manager," he added when Nikki's eyes widened at this sign of laxity in him. "Whenever I need to hire someone—whenever anyone in the family needs to hire someone—Claire takes care of all the initial interviewing and . . ." he made a limp-wristed, brushing-away motion with his hand, deliberately trying to provoke her with a show of aristocratic disdain for all the mundane little details of life " . . . reference checks and whatever."

"Cute," Nikki said, refusing to rise to the bait. She pushed her breakfast plate away to make room for the reports. "It looks like Bill's people did a thorough job. As usual," she commented as she laid the folders in front of her. There were six separate reports, each of varying thicknesses, each held in its own file folder. She looked across the table at Pierce, silently asking him if he was ready to proceed.

He sighed heavily. "I really, really hate this, you know?"

"I know," Nikki said, forgetting her antagonism for the moment in her effort to ease his obvious discomfort. "But it has to be done."

"It feels like I'm . . . I don't know . . . like I'm violating their trust."

"You don't have to read them," Nikki offered. "I'll read them. And if there's something you should know, I'll tell you."

Pierce shook his head. "That would be even worse, somehow. Like letting someone else do my dirty work for me so I can pretend I wasn't involved." He got up and pulled his chair over next to hers. "We'll read them together."

She waited until he'd poured himself another cup of coffee, flipping through the reports to find the one that would cause him the least distress. Prying into a person's private life was easier if you didn't know the person personally.

"Here. This one's on the pool maintenance people," she said, placing it on top of the stack. "M&E Pool Maintenance is owned and operated by two brothers, Miguel and Esteban Alvarez," she read, paraphrasing as she went. "They've been in business for over ten years and employ mostly college students in teams of two to do the actual work. There are two different teams that work on your pool on a fairly regular basis. One team is made up of two guys. The other team is a guy and a girl. One of Bill's operatives checked her out and—"

"Wait a minute. Checked her out? What exactly does that mean?"

"It means that someone called M&E Pool Maintenance and talked to—" she glanced down at the report "—Esteban Alvarez about her. They also interviewed a few of her neighbors. She's recently engaged and planning to get married this summer, plus she and her fiancé were out with his parents the night of the fire, so I think it's safe to cross her off our list of possible suspects."

"You mean that girl's—" he gestured at the report "—boss and neighbors talked to complete strangers about her? Just told them anything they wanted to know?"

"Yes, basically, that's exactly what they did. It's not as coldhearted as it sounds," Nikki added, half amused and half amazed that Pierce seemed to be so outraged by it all. Surely the life of a movie star wasn't that sheltered? "I don't know exactly what approach the interviewers used. It isn't noted in the report. But the people being interviewed probably thought they were talking to an insurance adjuster or a loan officer or . . . I don't know . . . maybe the interviewer came right out and admitted to doing a background check. A good interviewer tends to go with whatever he or she thinks will work."

"Do you do that kind of thing?" He nodded toward the reports.

Nikki shook her head. "I'm not a good interviewer," she said, and shifted the report on M&E Pool Maintenance to the bottom of the stack. She flipped open the next folder. "Maids For You," she said, and skimmed through the information Bender Security had compiled on the various people who had helped Mrs. Gilmore clean Pierce's house over the past year. She read bits and pieces of it aloud, noting, finally, that there were four among the staff of Maids For You whose exact whereabouts the night of the fire couldn't be verified by Bill Bender's investigators. "Two of them are Latinas, neither of whom read or write English, although both of them speak it a little. One got married and moved away. The other one quit the service the day before the fire and hasn't been heard from since. Not uncommon in the business, apparently. She's a long shot, but Bill thinks it's worth persuing. At least for a while. He assigned an operative to track her down."

Folder two was shuffled to the bottom of the stack.

"Janice Bressler," Nikki read, flipping open the next folder. "Started her own lawn service company five years ago after a very nasty divorce in which her husband managed to get just about everything. She has three children. Two boys, sixteen and fourteen, who help her with the business when they're not in school, and a ten-year-old girl. She started back to school last year to get her degree in landscape design. Sounds like she'd be way too busy to run around after you with her tongue hanging out, doesn't it?" Nikki commented, flashing a teasing look at Pierce from under her eyelashes.

He scowled at her.

"The report includes some samples of her company stationery. Letterhead. Invoices. Notepaper. It's similar," she commented, referring to the paper the fan letters had been written on, "but I'd say it's more of a dusty blue than pastel blue, wouldn't you?" she asked, handing Pierce a sheet of the notepaper to look at for himself.

He laid it down on the table without comment.

"I'd be inclined to discount her as a suspect," Nikki said then, "except for the way she looks at you when she thinks no one's watching. And the fact that the investigator couldn't find out exactly where she was on the night of the fire. She hired a baby-sitter for her daughter that night and supposedly went out on a date."

"Supposedly?"

"No one actually saw the date. If there was one, she might have met him somewhere rather than have him pick her up at her house. Bill's going to have someone keep an eye on her to see if we can find out anything more concrete."

"Oh, my God," Pierce said, appalled at what he considered the invasion of an innocent woman's privacy.

Nikki reached over and patted his hand. "We're almost finished," she said soothingly.

"And the worst is yet to come."

"Mrs. Marjorie Gilmore," she said, quickly perusing the file. "Nothing incriminating here."

"Thank God," Pierce said.

"She was born in Bloomington, Minnesota. One sister, Barbara, mother of Lisbeth. She married an army drill sergeant when she was nineteen. Well," Nikki muttered to herself, "that explains why she always makes me feel like a raw recruit. Let's see, she was widowed fifteen years ago and has been working as a housekeeper ever since. Excellent references. Excellent work record." She put the report aside. "If it wasn't for the fact that she was here on the night of the fire, she wouldn't even be on our list of suspects," Nikki said, and picked up the fourth file folder.

"Lisbeth Greene," she read aloud, glancing at Pierce to see how he was holding up. He seemed to be fine. Disgruntled but fine. "Only child of Dr. and Mrs. Greene. Born in Edina, Minnesota, a wealthy suburb of Minneapolis. She was a high achiever all through high school. Honor roll, pom-pom squad, student government, drama club. She apparently had some trouble with anorexia during the last two years of high school. She was hospitalized for it once, and she and her mother—but not doctor dad, apparently—went regularly to a family therapist. After high school, she enrolled at the University of Minnesota but dropped out after six months—oh, this is interesting."

"I don't think I like that tone of voice," Pierce said.

"There was some trouble with one of her teachers. A male teacher," Nikki said, giving him a significant look from under her lashes. "She says they had an affair. He claims it was all in her mind." She read a little further. "Oh, Lord, that poor girl."

"What?"

"She tried to commit suicide by taking an overdose of barbiturates. Her mother found her before it was too late and rushed her to emergency. She was seeing a psychiatrist twice a week until last fall, when she transferred out here to go to school." Nikki closed the report. "I hate to say it after all the problems she's already had in her life, but it looks as if she's still our most likely suspect. She does seem to have quite a few problems with the male figures in her life. Starting, I suspect," she said, tapping the folder with her finger, "with her father."

"Thank you, Dr. Freud."

"I'm not saying she's absolutely the one. In fact, right now, Janice Bressler is as much of a suspect. But I am saying we need to keep an eye on her. Surely you can see the logic in that?"

Pierce sighed. "Unfortunately, yes, I can." He propped his elbows on the table and dropped his head into his hands, covering his eyes for a moment. "Are we almost finished with this?"

"Just one more," Nikki said. "Kathy Frye." She paused to take a sip of her cooling coffee before opening the folder. "Hmm," she said after a moment, "this is interesting."

"I don't think I want to hear this. You thought the last report was interesting, too."

"Not ominous interesting," Nikki assured him. "Just interesting interesting. Kathy used to be an actress. Her stage name was Cherie Bombe. B-O-M-B-E. Does that ring a bell?"

Pierce thought about it for a second. "Nope. I can't say that it does. Maybe Claire would recognize it. She seems to remember the name of anyone who ever worked in Hollywood."

"Well, it was nearly twenty-five years ago. Obviously, her career never went anywhere or she'd still be—oh, my," Nikki said, and slapped the photograph she'd just picked up facedown on the table.

"Now I *know* I don't want to hear this," Pierce said, reacting more to the shock in her voice than her abrupt action.

"My offer still stands," Nikki said. "I'll take it to my room and finish reading it by myself, if you want."

Pierce shook his head and reached out to pick up the photograph. Very reluctantly, he turned it over.

It was a black-and-white publicity still of a very voluptuous young woman in her late teens. Despite the long blond hair, exaggerated makeup and black leather peekaboo outfit, complete with thigh-high boots and a whip, it was undoubtedly the woman they knew as Kathy Frye.

Pierce put the picture facedown on the table. "Judging from that, I'd say she must have done porno flicks."

"*Vixen With A Whip. Lady Dangerous. Cherry Delight*," Nikki read the movie titles from the report. "There are about a dozen more. It looks like she did the last one over...let's see—" Nikki mentally counted backward "—over twenty years ago. After that, noth-

ing. Cherie Bombe completely disappeared from sight.
Three years later Kathy Frye went to work as a recep-
tionist at a casting agency. She worked as an extra for
a while, too, under the name of Kay Fielding. All le-
gitimate films," Nikki said, "but it looks like she never
really caught on. She quit acting altogether in—" she
ran her finger down the list "—it looks like her last role
was a good sixteen years ago. After that she went to
work for Universal as a secretary. A very good secretary, apparently, since she stayed there for nearly fourteen years. She quit Universal to go to work for you."
Nikki paused, her head tilted consideringly. "That
seems a bit strange, don't you think, to quit a company
after fourteen years?"

"Not if you consider that I'm probably paying her
twice what Universal was."

"Are you?"

Pierce raised an eyebrow.

"Paying her twice what Universal was?"

"You'll have to ask Claire that question. She takes
care of all the bills." He looked down at the file con-
taining the report on his secretary. "Does this mean
Kathy goes to the top of the list of suspects?"

"Not necessarily," Nikki said. "Not because of this,
anyway. But it doesn't mean that we mark her off, either," she warned him. "She's still one of the few people who has access to the details of your private life. She
was here on the night of the fire. And she started working for you about the same time the letters started ar-
riving, give or take a month. That's enough to keep her
name on the list as far as I'm concerned."

Pierce sighed. "When this is all over, I want you to
destroy that report," he said. "Burn it. And I want you
to get in touch with Bill Bender and tell him to do the

same thing. I want every copy destroyed, especially the pictures. No matter what happens, Kathy must never know that we know about that." He flicked a hand at the picture lying facedown on the table between them. "She's obviously worked very hard to put her past behind her and make something good out of her life. I think that past should stay where it is. Agreed?"

"Agreed," Nikki said. She gathered all the materials together and stood up. "I'll go call Bill."

"IS IT REALLY NECESSARY to have lunch in the Polo Lounge?" Nikki asked as they pulled up in front of the Beverly Hills Hotel. "Couldn't we have eaten at home?"

"We could have," Pierce said as he put the Lamborghini into Park, "but I wanted to get out of the house for a while." He tossed the keys at the valet and took Nikki's arm to lead her into the lobby.

"Other side, please," she said, slipping around behind his back, so that her right hand was free.

Pierce frowned at her, disliking the reminder that she was wearing a gun under her bright red blazer.

"You were the one who wanted to get out," she reminded him with a wide grin. "So stop sulking. It's very unbecoming. And smile, darling," she said as they swept into the star-studded Polo Lounge.

The maître d' hurried over to greet them. "Right this way, please, Mr. Kingston," he said, bowing slightly. "We have your usual table ready for you."

Nikki felt as if every eye in the place were on them as they crossed the gallery. Or on Pierce, anyway. And she couldn't blame them. Dressed in one of his brand-new outfits, he was definitely a sight to see. A tall, golden Greek god, splendidly turned out in Calvin Klein's latest version of men's casual wear—white linen box-pleated trousers with a woven leather belt, a cream silk-knit Henley shirt, a linen blazer in a color called "natural" and a pair of Mexican leather sandals worn without socks. Or one Mexican leather sandal, anyway; his left heel and ankle were cradled in the heavy canvas and plastic of his cast.

Only a man as naturally beautiful and elegant as Pierce Kingston could manage to look so damned debonair and sophisticated in pure linen, Nikki thought as she strolled along beside him to their table. When she wore linen, the only look she seemed able to achieve was wrinkled.

It was undoubtedly those Kingston genes again; they had to be one of the great mysteries of the universe.

"Thank you, Craig," Pierce said to the maître d' and motioned for Nikki to slide into the booth. "Would you have the waiter bring us a bottle of champagne," he asked, naming a vineyard and a vintage that had the maître d' smiling in approval. "And a bowl of fresh strawberries, please."

"Very good, sir," the maître d' said, and went away.

"Is that all I get for lunch?" Nikki asked. "You make me get dressed up like a store mannequin—" she indicated the stark white silk tank top and sarong skirt she was wearing under her red blazer "—and all I get out of it is strawberries and champagne?"

"Strawberries and champagne and…" He paused on the brink.

"And?" she asked, looking up at him expectantly.

It was the opening he'd been waiting for, the reason he'd wanted to get her out of the house. "And kisses," he said, turning his words into action.

His mouth captured hers for a long, sweet moment. Lightly, playfully, asking for nothing more than the giddy pleasure of a stolen kiss. *At this rate*, thought Nikki, *I'm going to be too far gone to appreciate the champagne.*

"We had a deal," she said when he finally raised his mouth from hers.

"We still have a deal."

"If I remember it rightly, our deal was that everything was going to be strictly business between us." She skewed him with a look. "That didn't feel very businesslike."

"Didn't it?" Pierce said, feigning shock. "I must be losing my touch. It was supposed to be very businesslike." He leaned closer to her, putting his lips to her ear. "If you'll recall, sweetheart, part of our business arrangement was that we're supposed to convince my public that we're lovers, remember? Ah, Craig—" he straightened as the maître d' returned with the champagne. "You brought it yourself. Thank you."

Nikki waited silently while the maître d' opened the champagne, filled their flutes and snuggled the bottle down into the silver ice bucket.

"After everything that's been in the tabloids lately, I don't think anyone needs convincing on that score," she said when the maître d' moved away from the table.

Pierce shook his head, his eyes sparkling at her over the rim of his champagne glass. "It's obvious you don't understand Hollywood," he chided her as he set his glass down on the heavy linen tablecloth. "If we just sit here, talking in a calm and businesslike manner with no billing and cooing, some reporter's going to write that the romance of the decade has gone into a deep freeze." He took another sip of his champagne. "Someone might even print that we were overheard discussing the details of the palimony agreement."

"Billing and cooing?"

"An old Hollywood term for making out. Ah, here comes the waiter with our strawberries. Quick, kiss me," he said, and leaned forward to capture her lips again, just as the waiter set a crystal bowl of plump red strawberries on the table.

He tasted of champagne and sunlight and something, Nikki thought, that was uniquely him. She was smiling when he lifted his lips from hers.

"You're a scandalous rogue, Pierce Kingston," she said, but there was no censure in her voice.

He gave her his pirate's grin. "And you love it."

Yes, Nikki thought, and in that instant everything was suddenly made blindingly clear to her. *Yes, I love it. And you. I love you.* How could she not have realized it sooner? How could she not have seen it coming and done something—anything—to protect herself against it? She, Nikki Antonia Martinelli, bodyguard and ex-leatherneck, was in love with another pretty face. And this time he was the reigning heartthrob of the silver screen. *Oh, dear.*

"Here." He plucked a bright red strawberry out of the bowl and popped it between her open lips, totally unaware of the cataclysm going on inside her. "Have a strawberry. And then take a sip of champagne. The flavors enhance each other. I learned that from *Pretty Woman*," he admitted ingenuously, his smile inviting her to smile with him.

He meant for this to be a lighthearted afternoon, with no thoughts of crazy fans or fires or thinly veiled death threats. Or wondering if someone he knew was really behind it all. There would be no tying himself up in knots, forcing himself to keep his hands off his bodyguard, either, because here, in public, she was his to touch and kiss and romance to his heart's content.

He'd never really romanced a woman before, not in the sense of wooing a reluctant woman into his arms and his bed. The women he'd known before Nikki had never been reluctant. Coy, sometimes, to add spice to the chase, but never truly reluctant. The sensation was an interesting one. A mite frustrating, but interesting, all the same. It made the thought of her eventual surrender all the sweeter. All the hotter. Because, when this was over, she *would* surrender to him. She'd surrender everything.

"You're not drinking your champagne," he said. "Don't you like it? Should I order a different kind?"

"No, it's fine."

"But?"

"But I'm working."

"Oh, jeez, still?" He made it a comic refrain, pouting just a bit, like a spoiled little boy who wasn't getting his own way by being charming and was wondering if throwing a tantrum would help.

Nikki eyed him warily, not at all sure it was just an act put on for her benefit.

He sighed. Heavily. "Okay," he said. "No champagne." He motioned the waiter over. "Take this away," he said grandly, indicating the bottle of champagne, "and bring us a bottle of your best ginger ale."

"And menus," Nikki said in a strangled voice, trying not to laugh. "I'm hungry."

"And menus," Pierce said to the waiter. "The lady says she's hungry." He picked up Nikki's hand and brought it to his lips. "The gentleman is hungry, too," he said, and pretended to gnaw on her knuckles.

"Very good, sir," the waiter said, deadpan, as if he were quite used to seeing the male clientele of the Polo Lounge nibble on their female luncheon companions.

The afternoon continued in the same lighthearted vein after that. Kisses and silly conversation were interspersed with bites of grilled chicken breasts with a honey-mustard sauce and baby vegetables dressed with olive oil and herbs. They had more strawberries for dessert, with whipped cream this time, and tiny cups of double-strength espresso. It was late afternoon when they finally left the hotel, sated with good food and easy laughter, feeling at peace with the world.

"I'm really sorry, Mr. Kingston," the valet said when he came back from the parking lot without Pierce's Lamborghini. "I don't know how it could have happened."

"How what happened?"

"I'm sure the hotel will be willing to pay for the damage."

"Oh, jeez. Did someone sideswipe my car?"

"No, sir. It's right over there, sir," the valet indicated the Lamborghini's position on the lot with a nervous sweep of his arm. "I don't know how it could have happened," he said again. "It's never happened before," he assured them as Pierce and Nikki hurried over to where the car was parked.

All four of the Lamborghini's tires had been slashed.

There was a piece of paper tucked under the windshield wiper, like a note left behind when the damage has been accidental and the perpetrator has enough of a conscience to leave his phone number and insurance information. The paper was pale blue. Nikki leaned over and plucked it out from under the wiper.

"I hope your little afternoon love fest was worth it," she read aloud. *"Next time it will be you."*

All the blood drained from Nikki's face. "Oh, God," she said, knowing that the author of the note was insinuating that, the next time, she intended to use the knife on Pierce. "Oh, dear God."

She put her left hand on Pierce's back, pushing him toward the entrance to the hotel, reaching under her jacket with her right hand to touch the reassuring bulk of the 9mm Baretta nestled in the shoulder holster under her arm.

"Nikki, damn it, wait a minute," he said, automatically resisting her. "What the hell are you doing?"

"Please, Pierce." She pushed him harder. "Don't argue with me now. We've got to get you inside where it's safe."

11

NIKKI AGONIZED all the way home in the taxi, chastising herself for exposing Pierce to danger, telling herself she should have resisted his blandishments and insisted that they stay behind the closed gates of the estate. What if the culprit hadn't been content with just slashing the tires on Pierce's car? What if she'd come inside the restaurant after him? What if she'd been carrying a gun instead of knife?

Next time it will be you.

Her mind raced on at a mile a minute, trying to analyze the true extent of the danger and figure out what form it would take the next time. Her instincts were on autopilot, automatically monitoring the traffic as it flowed around the taxi, checking out the occupants of each car that passed them, tensing each time the taxi slowed or stopped. A backfire split the air and she grabbed Pierce's arm with both hands, intent on dragging him down on the seat, out of the line of fire. She released him in the next instant, realizing that the sound hadn't been a gunshot. Pierce reached over, totally oblivious to what she had intended to do, and covered her knee with his hand. "You okay?"

Nikki gritted her teeth. "Fine."

"Well, try to relax a little." He gave her a reassuring smile and a caressing little pat on the knee. "We'll be home in a few minutes."

Did the man have ice water in his veins? Or didn't he understand that his life was in danger?

Next time it will be you.

Just remembering the words written on that pale blue piece of paper sent a cold shiver down Nikki's spine. *Who is it?* she wondered, sifting through all the possibilities in her mind. *Damn it, who?*

It had to be someone who knew they were going to be at the Polo Lounge, she decided. Someone who knew Pierce's luncheon plans. The only two people who'd been at the estate when they left were Kathy Frye and Marjorie Gilmore.

Then again, the Lamborghini's tires could have been slashed by someone who'd followed them from Pierce's Beverly Hills estate to the hotel. Someone who'd been waiting outside the now-barred gates for just such an opportunity. Janice Bressler, maybe. Or that woman from the cleaning service Bill's investigators still hadn't been able to trace. Or Lisbeth Greene, who hadn't been to visit her aunt since the fire.

The culprit could also have been someone who just happened to see the car in the parking lot of the Beverly Hills Hotel. A red Lamborghini wasn't all that unusual in Southern California, certainly, but it was eye-catching, and Nikki would bet there was only one with a pair of fuzzy white baby booties hanging from the rearview mirror. Someone who wasn't even on their list of suspects could have recognized the car and the booties and realized her quarry must be inside the hotel with his new lover.

The culprit could be anyone.

Anyone at all.

Which meant the danger was everywhere.

Nikki turned to the man sitting beside her in the back seat of the taxi. "Do you have someplace you can go?" she asked, low. "Someplace where no one would ever think to look for you?"

"My family has a cabin at Mammouth," he answered in the same soft whisper she'd used to ask the question. "Why?"

"And no one knows about it? Not the press or your friends or anyone?"

"Just the family."

"And it's absolutely safe?"

"As safe as anyplace can be, I guess. Why do you—" And then it hit him. "Oh, no. No. You can just forget that idea. I'm not going into hiding. That's totally out of the question."

"Damn it, Pierce, your life is more important than that macho movie-star reputation of yours!"

"No," he said again. "And that's absolutely final."

"But why?" It was a cry directly from her frightened heart.

"Because if I went into hiding I'd be doing the very thing I've fought against all my life." He reached out and took both of her hands in his, turning sideways on the seat to face her. "I was six months old when I appeared in my first movie," he said in explanation. "My father was directing a film with Sophia Loren and they decided they needed a baby in one scene, and since I was on the set with my mother . . ." He shrugged. "The point is, I've been in the limelight practically since the day I was born. There are very few places I can go without attracting attention. There are some places I can't go without attracting a mob. It's something you learn to deal with if you plan to stay in this business very long, and my way of dealing with it has always

been to ignore it as much as I can. And that means refusing to live my life behind an electrified fence, surrounded by an entourage to insulate me from the world
any more than I already am. That's why I won't go into
hiding, Nikki. Not because of the damage it might do
to my reputation, but because I refuse to let anyone put
any more restrictions on me than there already are. And
because, if I do, then she's won."

"Not even for a little while?" Nikki said. "Not just
until this woman is caught?"

"Who's to say she'll ever be caught? And how are you
going to catch her, anyway—" he lifted one hand and
touched her nose lightly with the tip of his finger "—if
you haven't got me for bait?"

"Don't joke about it, please. It isn't the least bit
funny."

"I wasn't joking, sweetheart," he said as the taxi
pulled up in front of the gates to his estate. "I was just
stating a simple fact. There's no way to smoke this
woman out without me, because I'm what triggers her
to do what she does." He leaned over to reach for the
window controls.

"No," Nikki said, stopping him. "You stay right
there." She would have liked to tell him to get down on
the seat, but she had a pretty good idea of how that
would be received. She lowered the window on her side
and leaned out of the car to press the intercom button
on the pole-mounted control panel.

"Yes, who is it, please?" said a voice in answer to her
buzz, and then, as whoever it was recognized her on the
monitor. "Oh, Nikki, it's you."

Nikki tensed. The voice didn't sound familiar.

"How come you didn't use the transmitter in Pierce's
car?" the voice asked. "Is it broken?"

"Lisbeth?" Nikki said, finally recognizing the voice coming over the intercom. What was Lisbeth doing here? When had she arrived? How long had she been here? And why had she asked about the car? Had they left danger behind only to find it waiting for them again at home?

There was just one way to find out, and staying here wasn't it. "We left the car at the hotel and took a taxi home," Nikki said.

"Why—"

"It's a long story." She cut the young woman off before she could finish asking. "Just buzz us in, please," she said, and released the button. "Lisbeth's here," she said to Pierce.

The taxi started up the wide curving driveway.

"So?" said Pierce.

"So, she hasn't been to visit her aunt since the night of the fire. What's she doing here now?"

"Visiting her aunt?" Pierce guessed.

"On the very day there's another assault on you? Doesn't that strike you as the least bit suspicious?"

"Nikki, sweetheart, she's here and we were there," he pointed out with infuriating logic. "How can that be suspicious?"

"It depends," Nikki said darkly as the taxi circled the topiary garden and pulled to a stop in front of the wide stone steps, "on just how long she's been here. Pay the man," she said, and slid out of the taxi.

She positioned herself between Pierce and the front door, not really expecting trouble from anyone inside but prepared for it nonetheless. She'd been lax up to now, letting Pierce's relaxed charm and unconcerned savoir faire lull her into letting things slide.

That was about to change.

They went up the front steps together and stood there for a moment, at Nikki's insistence, watching the taxi until it disappeared through the gates.

"Don't you think you're taking this just a tad too far?" Pierce asked as she opened the front door and went directly to the monitor panel to press the button that would close the gates. "You can't suspect everyone of trying to do me bodily harm."

"Yes," Nikki said. "I can." She closed the door, throwing the dead bolt lock into place with a flick of her wrist and a significant look at the man standing beside her. "And you have no idea how far I can take it."

She moved away from him and the door, the soles of her strappy white Farigamo sandals slapping against the black-and-white marble tiles of the foyer as she headed for the kitchen. There was determination in every step she took.

"What are you up to?" Pierce asked, following along behind her.

She didn't pause. "You'll see."

"No." He grabbed her arm, stopping her in her tracks. "I won't see. I want you to tell me."

Nikki tried to yank her arm out of his long-fingered grasp, couldn't, and immediately stopped the useless effort. She could have freed herself, and quite easily, if she'd been willing to take advantage of his injured leg. Which she wasn't. She glared at him instead, her green eyes flashing sparks that promised all sorts of madness and mayhem if he didn't let her go.

He glared right back, not the least bit intimidated by her glowering expression. "Neither of us is moving one inch from this spot until you calm down and tell me just exactly what you're up to."

"What I'm up to is my job," Nikki shot back. "The one Kingston Productions hired me to do and the one you've been doing your level best to keep me from doing properly."

"How have I kept you from doing your job?" Pierce demanded. "I've agreed to the monitor at the gate, haven't I? And the panic button by my bed? I've agreed to the dogs patrolling the grounds at night. And those damned reports. I agreed to those, didn't I?"

"Half measures," Nikki accused.

"What the hell else do you want?"

"I want motion detectors along the perimeter of the wall and alarms on all the exits and entrances, including windows. I want this estate to be off-limits to anyone who might be a suspect, and I want the right to question those suspects as I see fit. I want you to stay in this house under a twenty-four-hour guard. And I want a limousine with bullet-proof glass and a chauffeur trained in evasive driving techniques for those times when you absolutely have to go out. But most of all," she said, her breath coming hard and fast in her agitation, "what I want is for you to start taking this whole thing seriously."

"I'll give you the motion detectors on the perimeter," Pierce said, entranced by the utter magnificence of her feminine fury, "and the limousine with the bullet proof glass, but that's all."

"Damn it, Pierce! This isn't some movie you're in. It's real life. *Your* life. And you're in real danger. Why can't you understand that?"

"I understand it," he said quietly. "I understand it much better than you think. But what *you* have to understand is that I meant what I said in the taxi. I'm not going to let it govern the way I live my life. I'll put up with the alarms and the guards since you seem to think they're so necessary. I'll even try to restrict my movements to make myself less of a target—for a while, anyway. But what I won't put up with, what I absolutely refuse to condone, is accusing anyone of anything without proof. I'm not about to allow you to grill my staff, or anyone else as if they were convicted felons. Neither will I ban anyone from this house because of something they *might* be guilty of."

"And if someone tries to murder you in your sleep again?"

"That someone will have to get past those alarms of yours first, won't she?"

"Pierce!"

"That's absolutely my final word on it." His stare was as uncompromising as a stone wall. "Take it or leave it."

Nikki thought about it for about ten seconds. She was sorely tempted to leave it. To just walk away, then and there, instead of continuing to try to protect him with one hand tied behind her back. But she couldn't. "All right," she snarled, and jerked her arm out of his hold. "But I'm getting those motion detectors installed tomorrow," she threatened, and stalked off down the hall to the kitchen.

Pierce let out a breath he hadn't even known he'd been holding. He didn't know what he would have done if she'd taken the other option. Probably promised to put himself in solitary confinement and let her have the key to his cell. *No*, he thought, his pirate's grin beginning to curve his lips as he followed her furiously twitching hips down the hall. He'd have promised to put himself in solitary confinement if she went with him. And then thrown away the key.

"BUT WHY IS THE PREMIERE of *The Devil's Game* so all-fired important?" Nikki asked for what seemed like the tenth time. She intended to keep asking until she got a satisfactory answer. "The film's going to be shown to-night whether you go or not. People have already pur-chased their tickets," she argued. "So I don't see how your not going can affect—"

"Movie," Pierce said as he handed her a champagne flute filled with ginger ale.

"What?"

"Movie," Tara said, and reached out to accept the glass her brother-in-law held out to her. "Ingmar Berg-man makes films."

"Pronounced with two syllables," Gage put in.

Tara smiled at him. "Fil-ums," she said obediently, the wide skirts of her taffeta gown rustling softly as she sat down on the chintz sofa with her ginger ale. "Kingston Productions makes movies."

"There's a difference?" Nikki asked.

Pierce looked at the ceiling. "The woman's a hea-then," he said to no one in particular. "Fil-ums," he ex-plained to Nikki, "are full of literary symbolism and deep meaning. They're meant to educate and enlighten the audience." He took a sip of champagne. "Movies, on the other hand, are meant to entertain them."

"That's very interesting," she said. "But it still doesn't tell me why it's so important that you attend this par-ticular movie premiere."

"Well." He stuck his hands into his pants pockets and ducked his head modestly, lifting his wide shoulders in an aw-shucks shrug. "I *am* the star," he said, looking up at her from under his lashes. "Isn't that reason enough?"

"No," Nikki said bluntly.

Gage lifted an eyebrow at his brother. "Tenacious, isn't she?"

Pierce grinned. "One of her many charms."

Nikki gritted her teeth. "Pierce," she said warningly.

"Oh, go ahead and tell her," Gage said.

"Tell who, what?" Claire asked as she came into the garden room with a tall, tuxedoed young man trailing close behind her. She introduced him to Nikki as her administrative assistant, Robert.

"Pierce was just about to tell Nikki why it's so all-fired important that he be at the premiere of *The Devil's Game* tonight when she's already told him it's too much of a security risk," Gage said when the introductions were over.

Claire's lovely face clouded with concern. "*Is* it too much of a risk?"

"No," Pierce said.

"Yes," Nikki said at the same time.

"If you really think it—" Claire began.

"I'm going and that's final," Pierce said firmly. He looked at Nikki. "Why do I always find myself issuing ultimatums when I'm around you?" he asked, as if he were truly perplexed by a newly discovered phenomenon.

"Probably because you're an insensitive, pig-headed, macho jerk who doesn't know what's good for him."

"No, go ahead and tell him what you really think," Gage said. "Don't be shy around us."

Nikki blushed but the laughter was good-natured.

"I think you ought to tell her the truth," Claire said when it died down. "After all," she said dryly, nodding her thanks for the glass of champagne Gage handed to her, "you wouldn't want her to continue thinking of you as an insensitive jerk."

Nikki looked at Pierce expectantly.

"Well . . ." His broad shoulders shifted uneasily under the fine black material of his tuxedo jacket. "The truth is, I'm a little nervous about this one. Well, not this one but the next one."

Gage snickered into his champagne. "A little?"

Nikki ignored him. "Why?"

Pierce shrugged again, managing, somehow, to look endearingly sheepish. It was a side of him she'd never seen before. A very appealing side.

"Oh, for goodness' sake," Claire said. "You'd think you were confessing to doing a remake of *Heaven's Gate*. The reason he—" she motioned toward her brother with the champagne glass in her hand "—is so insistent on attending this premiere is the same reason he's been so insistent on doing all the extra publicity for *The Devil's Game*," she said. "His next project is going to be a romantic comedy—completely out of character for him. Well," she admended, "out of character with the character he usually plays. Actually the character of Matt Gleason is going to be a lot more like the real Pierce than anything he's ever done before."

"Which is what's making him so nervous," said Gage.

Nikki looked back and forth between Pierce's siblings. "I don't understand."

"That's because neither one of them knows what the hell they're talking about," Pierce growled.

Claire ignored him. "He thinks he needs to build up as much career momentum on this movie as possible in case the next one's a bomb. Which it won't be," she said, and flashed a triumphant smile at her brother. "As of 1:12 p.m. this afternoon," she announced, "Penny Marshall has agreed to direct."

Pierce's lips turned up in a blinding smile of boyish delight. "You did it," he exulted, and saluted her with his glass. "You said you would."

"Excuse me," Marjorie Gilmore said from the door as glasses were being raised all around in acknowledgment of Claire Kingston's latest coup. "The car has arrived."

Pierce looked at the thin gold watch on his wrist. "Right on time," he said, and put down his unfinished glass of champagne. "We'd better get going."

"A few minutes more won't hurt—" Claire began, and then laughed. "Oh, all right. Let's go before he starts to pout."

As everybody put down their glasses and got to their feet to begin the general exodus toward the door, Nikki suddenly became aware of one very glaring fact. She was amazed she hadn't noticed it before.

"What?" said Pierce, immediately catching her expression of discomfort.

Nikki looked back and forth between the other two women. Tara was resplendent in an amethyst gown of crisp taffeta with a low sweeping neckline that bared the creamy skin of her shoulders and the tops of her lush breasts. Claire was as elegant as a princess in a strapless ivory silk sheath with intricate, understated beadwork covering the bodice. "You're both wearing long dresses," she said.

"So?" Pierce said. "Is that a problem?"

"Oh, Pierce," said Claire, immediately understanding what Nikki meant. "Don't be so male."

Nikki's dress was a pale shiny green satin, the shade falling somewhere between lime sherbet and chartreuse, and almost an exact match for her unusual eyes. The style was simple with a high mandarin collar that emphasized the length of her neck and a narrow hem that stopped well above her knees, showcasing her chorus-girl legs. She wore a loose collarless jacket over it, almost as long as the dress itself, completely covered with iridescent paillettes that sparkled and shimmered with every movement of her body. Her gun and shoulder holster were under it.

"You look lovely," Claire said truthfully. "The dress is exquisite and so are you. Pierce has excellent taste."

"You're not just trying to be nice?"

"No, she's not just trying to be nice," Pierce said. "I really do have excellent taste." He hustled them out the door of the garden room and down the hall to the front door. "Now let's get this show on the road."

"Oh, I don't like this," Nikki said uneasily as the specially built stretch limousine pulled up to the front of the theater. The crowd was loud and rambunctious, forming a gauntlet on either side of the red velvet ropes that cordoned off a pathway across the sidewalk between the line of limousines and the front door. "I don't like this at all."

There was no way to protect a person in a crowd like this, not when you were a force of one just one person, Nikki fretted, watching the fans' frenzied reaction as each sleek automobile disgorged its famous passengers. She'd wanted to hire more bodyguards for the evening, enough to surround him and keep him reasonably safe in case anything happened, but Pierce wouldn't hear of it, so she'd secretly arranged for two of Bill Bender's best operatives to be part of the crowd. Every extra hand would help if an attempt was made on him tonight. And if Pierce didn't like what she'd done, so be it. He didn't have to like it.

The crowd sent up a loud cheer as Andie Mac-Dowell stepped out of the limousine just ahead of theirs. Pierce's leading lady waved and smiled, graciously acknowledging the enthusiastic accolades before disappearing into the theater. All eyes turned toward the last limousine. Nikki felt her stomach clench as the uniformed doorman leaned over to open the rear door. Cheers rose as she stepped out onto the sidewalk, then died down as the crowd realized she was nobody famous—although one or two avid tabloid readers called out her name. The noise surged again, politely, as first Gage, then Claire and, finally, her assistant—none of them readily recognizable faces—exited the limousine. It swelled much more enthusiastically when Tara appeared. She hadn't made a movie since *The Promise* two years ago, and she had vowed never to do another after she became pregnant with her first child, but the crowd remembered her. Mainly from her two-year stint as Jessica on the still-popular soap opera "As Time Goes By."

"We love you, Jessica," yelled somebody who obviously didn't know she was no longer on the show. Tara smiled sweetly and lifted her hand in a gracious wave.

There was an expectant eager hush; the crowd knew who to expect now. There was a sort of collective gasp, as if they were all holding their breaths, and then Pierce stepped out of the back seat of the limousine. Someone squealed. Someone else hollered his name. Applause broke out.

It was a movie premiere like movie premieres used to be in Hollywood's golden years, when movie stars were royalty and knew how to behave like it. Glamour and showmanship had been bred into Pierce Kingston from the cradle, fed to him through his mother's milk, honed through a lifetime of working on his craft. He smiled his twelve-million-dollar smile and raised his hand to acknowledge the accolades of the crowd.

They went wild, surging against the velvet ropes, screaming his name.

Nikki stayed close beside him as they began the slow trek across the pavement. Her gaze darted over the crowd, assessing it, looking for something unfamiliar, something out of the ordinary, something that would tell her what was going to happen a split second before it did. She fretted as Pierce ambled along at what seemed like a snail's pace to her, exchanging a word here and there, shaking a hand, signing autographs. She wanted to put her hand on his back and hurry him along, tell him to quit dawdling and get inside.

And then the velvet rope broke, or came loose from its mooring, and the crowd spilled forward, surrounding them, separating them. Nikki looked around wildly, trying to find her backup in the crowd, rudely elbowing her way back to Pierce's side. She had almost reached him when she saw something that triggered all her defensive reflexes. A slender figure, a bouncy brown shoulder-length bob, a hand reaching into a UCLA backpack and pulling out something long and...Nikki reached for her gun but the crowd was too thick to risk firing it. She shoved it back into her shoulder holster before it had cleared leather.

"Pierce!" she screamed. *"Pierce!"*

She launched herself in a flying tackle, knocking his would-be assailant off her feet with a brutal body check, and threw herself at Pierce with enough force to take him down, covering his body with hers as they fell.

One of the undercover operatives grabbed the young woman and hauled her roughly to her feet, yanking her weapon out of her hand. It was a black marking pen, over six inches long but not considered especially lethal.

Nikki struggled to her knees beside Pierce's supine body, unaware, at first, that she had attacked an innocent autograph seeker. All of her attention was focused on the man lying on his back on the length of red carpet that had been stretched over the sidewalk. His face was screwed up in a horrible grimace of pain.

Had he been hit, after all? Was he hurt?

And then, suddenly, he burst out laughing. "Oh, Nikki," he said, between whoops of uncontrollable laughter. "Nikki." He reached up and wrapped his arms around her, pulling her back down on top of him, oblivious to the stares of the fascinated spectators standing all around them. "You're priceless, do you know that? Utterly priceless."

She struggled in his embrace, fear turning to anger and then embarrassment as she realized what must have happened. "Pierce, damn it, let me up, you jackass," she demanded, as flashbulbs began to pop all around them. "The photographers are taking pictures of my underwear."

12

"I'M STILL NOT SURE this is a good idea," Nikki fretted as she pulled the specially built bullet-proof car to a stop in front of Claire's office bungalow. "There seem to be an awful lot of people just wandering around here."

"You can cover me with that cannon under your arm until I'm inside the door," Pierce said, humoring her.

"You're sure it's just Claire and her assistant inside?"

"That's it."

"And no one else is expected?"

"Jeez, Nikki, I don't know who might or might not have business with Claire. She's a very busy woman. But there's a guard at the gate. That man in the little house who made us show him our IDs before he'd let us on the lot? Remember? It's his job to see that no one's allowed access without authorization. But if anyone gets by him and storms Claire's office, I promise to hide in the bathroom, okay?"

Nikki sighed. "I know I sound paranoid. And you probably think it's excessive, especially after the way I overreacted last night, but it's my—"

"Your job," he said dryly. "I know. And you're doing it splendidly."

Nikki eyed him warily, unsure whether to be amused or annoyed by his tone. He was being patronizing, but in a very sweet way. And she owed him some slack after last night; he'd been very sweet about that, too. The hubbub in front of the theater had almost overshadowed what had gone on inside it. As far as the morning's tabloid headlines were concerned, it *had* overshadowed it. "All right. I'll leave you to discuss business with your sister. But you have to promise to call me as soon as you and Claire are finished. Okay?"

"Scout's honor," he said, neglecting to mention that he'd never been a Scout.

She glanced down at Pierce's leg. "Maybe I should just make sure you get up those steps all right," she said, loath to let him out of her sight.

"It's only three steps," he assured her. "And there's a handrail if I begin to feel faint."

"If you feel faint you shouldn't even be—"

He put his hand over her mouth. "That was a joke," he said, his eyes warm with amusement. "My leg is fine. *I'm* fine." He slid his hand around to the back of her neck, threading his fingers through her short, feathery hair. "Kiss me goodbye," he demanded, and pulled her head toward his.

Nikki stiffened her neck muscles against him, just a second too late. And then his lips were on hers, warm and soft and wonderful, and she decided that making an issue out of one little kiss would be silly. Even if it did technically violate their deal.

"Have fun installing your alarms," he murmured against her mouth. And then he slid across the seat and was out of the car. "I'll call you when I'm ready for you to come get me," he said, deliberately rephrasing what she'd said to him. "Now, go."

But Nikki lingered for a few moments longer, watching him as he walked up the steps to his sister's office and disappeared inside, wondering what she was going to do when this job was over and she didn't have his safety as an excuse to spend every waking minute thinking about him anymore.

CLAIRE LOOKED UP from the papers spread out on her desk, ready to frown at whomever was entering her office unannounced. She smiled instead. "Where's your bodyguard?" she asked, looking beyond Pierce as he sauntered into the room with only the barest suggestion of a limp.

"I sent her home."

She did frown then. "Yeah, right. Nikki wouldn't willingly let you out of her sight for a minute." She fixed him with an expression that reminded him very much of the one his mother used to level at him when she'd caught him doing something he wasn't supposed to. "You snuck out, didn't you?"

"I did not," Pierce said, imbuing his words with a trace of righteous indignation. He dropped onto the gray brocade love seat that was the only piece furniture in his sister's elegant office that allowed of any degree of comfort. "Nikki agreed that I'm as safe here as I would be at home. Safer, really," he added with a grin, "after I pointed out that none of her prime suspects could get to me here."

"Prime suspects?"

"Mrs. Gilmore's niece, Lisbeth. And Kathy. And the gardener." His expression made it clear that he didn't share his bodyguard's suspicions. "I think someone from the pool maintenance company is one, too. Or was it the cleaning service?" He shook his head. "I can't remember." He waved an elegant hand dismissively. "It's not important except that it got me out of the house without her." He lifted his injured leg—a great deal sorer since last night—and placed his heel on the polished marquetry cocktail table in front of him. Elevating it seemed to dull the throbbing a bit. "Nikki dropped me off and went back to see about those damned alarms she's having installed in the house. I'm supposed to call her when I'm finished here."

"But you're not going to," Claire said, correctly reading his expression. She leveled another hard look at him, fully prepared to deliver a lecture on the importance of following the orders that had been issued for his safety. "What are you up to?"

Pierce opened his mouth to tell her and then closed it without speaking.

"Pierce?"

He shrugged and looked away. "Nothing," he mumbled. "Never mind."

"Pierce Barrymore Kingston," Claire said, amazed and delighted, "are you *blushing*?"

He looked up at her from under his lashes with a sheepish, uncertain smile, his chiseled cheekbones very definitely pink. "What would you say if I told you I was going over to Buccellati when I leave here?"

"Buccellati, huh?" Claire leaned back in her chair and crossed her arms. One perfectly made-up eyebrow arched as she considered him. "Thinking of buying her a little thank-you gift for services above and beyond the call of duty?"

"No," he growled, unamused by her amusement. "I'm thinking of buying her an engagement ring."

Claire's air of cynical amusement vanished instantly. She jumped up from behind her desk and hurried toward him. "Oh, Pierce! I'm so happy for you," she said, dropping down onto the love seat beside him. She leaned over and hugged him. "I was beginning to wonder if you were going to be as pigheaded about falling in love as Gage was." Her blue eyes gleamed with tenderness and amusement. "Do you remember how we had to badger him into admitting his feelings for Tara? Right here in this very office. Remember?"

"I remember."

"God, it was like pulling teeth just to get him to admit he was in love with her. And then he went around, growling at everyone like an injured grizzly before he finally tracked her down and convinced her to marry him." She smiled with wholehearted approval. "I'm so glad you're being more sensible."

"Then you think it's a good idea?"

"I think it's a *wonderful* idea."

"You don't think it's too soon?"

"Too soon?"

"We've only known each other a month," he said, unaware that, unlike all his other relationships, he knew the time frame of this one exactly.

Claire suppressed a smile as she reached out to cup his face in her palms. "All right. Out with it. What's the matter?"

"The truth?"

"Always the best policy."

He hesitated for a moment. "I'm scared," he blurted out gruffly, as uncomfortable as a twelve-year-old boy admitting to still being afraid of the dark.

Claire stared at him for a moment, nonplussed, and then burst out laughing.

Pierce's discomfort edged into indignation. "What's so damned funny?"

"You." She leaned forward to plant a quick kiss on his mouth. "The great love-'em-and-leave-'em Pierce Kingston," she said, shaking her head as if she couldn't quite believe it, "Mr. Macho Movie Star, heartthrob of the Western World, has finally found a woman who has him shaking in his shoes." She laughed again and dropped her hands from his face. "What's the matter? Are you afraid she'll say no?"

He grinned faintly at that. "She might. In fact, she probably will. At first. But I can change her mind," he said confidently, thinking of the way she reacted to his slightest touch. He knew women well enough to know that she was his, if he wanted her. And he wanted her. God, how he wanted her! But... "I don't know if I should." He sighed.

"Why not? Has she got some deep, dark secret in her past that's going to come back to haunt you or something?" Claire asked, only half-teasing.

"No. It really hasn't got anything to do with Nikki at all," he said. "It's..." He shrugged. "I don't know, it's..."

"It's what?" Claire prompted gently, recognizing the very real torment in her brother's voice.

"It's me. It's who I am. Who I've been." He looked into eyes that were the exact shape and color of his. Eyes that had shared his past and his upbringing. "What if what everyone's always said all these years is true, Claire? What if I really am exactly like the old man?"

Claire stared back at him, uncertain what he meant. "Like Dad? Like Dad, how?"

"Oh, come on, Claire. You know what I mean. He's been married what? Six? Seven times? He's had more mistresses and live-in lovers than either of us can count or remember."

"Yes. So?"

"So each and every time he swore he was in love." Pierce lifted his foot down off the cocktail table and got to his feet and began pacing, too agitated to sit still.

"That this time—whichever time it was—was it. The real thing. Forever and ever, amen. That's how I feel about Nikki. That she's it for me. The woman I want to spend the rest of my life with." He stopped pacing and looked down at his sister. "But what if I'm wrong, Claire? What if I fall out of love with her tomorrow or next week or next year? I don't want to hurt her. I don't want to hurt myself. But, damn it, I don't want to let her go, either."

Claire shook her head, wondering how anyone could be so blind to his own nature. "How many times have you been in love before now? Not just in lust—I know those are too numerous to count—but truly in love?"

"Well . . ." Pierce paused consideringly. "When I was fifteen I was in love with . . ." He shook his head. "No, that wasn't love, because I fell right out of it a year later when, ah—" When the twenty-three-year old actress playing his older sister in a movie had seduced him in her trailer, but he wasn't going to tell his sister about that. "Well, there was Chelsea Payne, the actress I did *Close Contact* with about eight years ago, remember? We were hot and heavy there for over a year." Which was still a record for him.

"And when she married that English playwright because you wouldn't make a commitment, how long did you mourn?"

"I don't know. About, ah . . ."

"Exactly," Claire said, when Pierce couldn't answer. "You don't remember because you didn't mourn. If you're honest with yourself you'll admit you were relieved to see the last of her. In fact, if I remember rightly—and I always do—you were dating someone else within the week. That doesn't sound like love to me."

"Exactly my point."

Claire sighed. "All right, forget love for a minute and just tell me this . . ." She fixed her brother with a gimlet stare. "Have you ever felt about any woman the way you feel about Nikki? Have you ever wanted to propose marriage to anyone else?"

"No," he said without hesitation. "Never."

"Well, there you are, then."

"There I am, what?"

Claire threw up her hands. "Nobody's *that* out of touch with their feelings," she said. "I think your problem is the same one Gage had when he fell in love with Tara. Plain, old, instinctive male skittishness. I've heard it's pretty common."

Pierce considered that. "You think?" he asked hopefully.

"Yes." Claire grinned at him. "I think."

"Well, then—" his perfectly chiseled lips curled up in a grin to match hers "—how about letting me borrow your car?"

"Buccellati?"

"Buccellati," he confirmed.

"And if I refuse?"

Pierce grinned. "Then I'll take a taxi and be in even more danger."

Claire sighed and dug her keys out of her purse. "If something happens and you get hurt out here by yourself," she said as she handed them to him, "I expect you to tell Nikki that you overpowered me and took them."

"Thanks, sis," he said, and headed for the door. It opened as he reached for the knob.

"Sorry to interrupt," Robert said, sticking his head inside the office. "But you asked me to let you know when the contracts from Stallone's agent arrived."

Claire stood up and motioned him into the room. "Just put them on my desk. I'll go over them right now."

Robert came into the room. "There's a package here for you, too," he said, holding a small box out to Pierce. "It's marked 'PERSONAL.'"

Pierce took it from his sister's assistant and tucked it under his arm without even glancing at it. "If Nikki calls for me while I'm gone," he said, "tell her I'm in the bathroom. I'll be back soon."

He tossed the package onto the passenger seat of the silver Jaguar as he got into the car, his mind on the appropriateness of diamonds versus colored stones as he exited the studio lot. The drive to the jewelry store, located in the Regent Beverly Wilshire Hotel, was a short one. In less than forty-five minutes, he was seated in a private room, trying to decide between a flawless eleven-carat diamond solitaire and a five-carat square-cut peridot set in platinum and surrounded by smaller diamonds.

"The solitaire is classic," pointed out the jeweler, eager for the higher price it would bring.

"But the peridot matches her eyes," countered Pierce. Besides, he had a sneaking suspicion that his intended bride would find an eleven-carat diamond a bit ostentatious. He left with the diamond-studded peridot in a little velvet box, nestled into the breast pocket of his raw silk Armani jacket.

He sat in the Jaguar for a moment after he left the store, admiring the engagement ring and trying to decide just when he would make his proposal. If he had his way, he wouldn't wait another day to get the ring on her finger. But Nikki had scruples about such things. If she wouldn't sleep with him while she was his body-guard, it was probably a sure bet that she wouldn't agree to marry him while in that capacity, either. And he couldn't fire her, he thought, grinning, or she'd sue him.

Maybe, if he agreed to a whole platoon of body-guards, he could convince her to resign.

Or, maybe, the fan would strike again in the next couple of days and it would all be over.

One could only hope.

He snapped the velvet box closed and put it back in his inside pocket, then reached out to turn the key in the ignition. The package on the seat caught his eye. He picked it up. It was small and rectangular, about the size of a child's shoe box. It was wrapped in plain brown paper and packaging tape, and the address label was neatly typed rather than being written in the flowing script he had half expected. It made a muffled thumping noise when he shook it.

He took the key out of the ignition, used the end of it to tear through the tape, and slipped it back into place. Grasping the body of the box in one hand, he lifted the lid with the other.

A charred Barbie doll lay nestled in the satin-lined box as if it were in a coffin. It was naked and its long black hair had been hacked off so that it was sticking up in tiny spikes all over the doll's head. The smell of burnt plastic was almost overpowered by the musky smell of the perfume it had been doused with. Horrified, Pierce stared down at the grisly doll for a long moment. There was something there . . . something he should be seeing . . . something beyond what he was seeing . . . .

And then, suddenly, he knew.

He threw the box onto the seat with a strangled oath of rage and fear and reached for the ignition. The car roared to life. Pierce slammed it into gear and screamed out of the parking lot as if Satan himself were after him.

NIKKI OPENED the kitchen door with her key, already annoyed that there had been no plain black pickup truck from Bender Security in the driveway. Her annoyance increased when she realized there was no one in the kitchen, either. Someone was always supposed to be monitoring the monitor.

"Hello?" she called, the heels of her cowboy boots thudding against the tiles of the kitchen. The sound changed, becoming sharper and then muffled and sharper again, as she strode across the plush burgundy-and-gold Brussels carpet that adorned the center of the hardwood floor in the massive dining room. "Hello? Mrs. Gilmore?" Her voice echoed hollowly back at her as she crossed the marble foyer and headed down the hall to the garden room. "Anybody? Is anyone ho—oh, hi, Kathy," she said, smiling. "Where is everyone?"

"I haven't seen Mrs. Gilmore since this morning," Kathy said. "I guess she must still be out doing the grocery shopping. Lisbeth was by the pool, studying, the last time I saw her."

"Oh?" Nikki said, trying to sound casual. She'd promised Pierce that she wouldn't reveal her suspicions to anyone outside of him and Bill Bender. "How long has she been here?"

"I'm not sure. I wasn't the one who let her in."

"Oh, well." Nikki shrugged. "I guess it's not that important. I'll ask Mrs. Gilmore later." She moved toward the windows overlooking the pool area as she spoke, unable to resist the urge to check on the girl. "I was expecting a couple of guys from Bender Security to be here by now," she said over her shoulder. "They were supposed to start work on the motion detectors in Pierce's room."

"Somebody named Dean called just a few minutes ago. He said there was a problem at another site and they'd be about an hour and a half late."

Nikki looked at her watch. "Damn, that's going to throw a monkey wrench into things, especially if Pierce gets finished earlier than he thought." She frowned thoughtfully, still staring out the window. "I don't see Lisbeth," she said. "Are you sure she's out there?"

Kathy came up to the window beside her. "She was sitting there at the first umbrella table," she said, pointing. There was a stack of books and papers there, but no Lisbeth. "Maybe she went into the cabana. The door's open."

"Maybe," Nikki said, uneasy without knowing why. Pierce was out of harm's way for the moment, safely ensconced in his sister's office. "I think I'll go check on her."

"I'll be in my office if you need me," Kathy said.

Nikki nodded absently and pushed open the glass door. Stepping outside, she started to pass by the umbrella table, then stopped, her eye caught by a flash of pastel blue. There was an entire pad of lined blue notepaper lying next to the stack of textbooks, exactly like that which had been used to write the threatening letters to Pierce. Either Lisbeth was completely innocent, Nikki thought, or her obsession was making her careless.

The deranged mind of a stalker was apt to work that way, becoming more and more convinced that the fantasy it had created was true, until it was so real to the person who created it that she forgot it *was* just a fantasy. And that's when she became the most dangerous. Because she believed the world she had fabricated in her head was the real one.

What was Lisbeth doing in the cabana?

Nikki felt the hair on the back of her neck stand up. Something was wrong, she was sure of it. Something was terribly wrong. She slid her right hand under her jacket, feeling for the butt of her gun, and crept toward the open door, wishing she was wearing tennis shoes instead of the cowboy boots that practically announced her approach. Wishing for backup, too, while she was at it.

She should have insisted on armed guards and dogs for the daylight hours, too, she thought, at least until the alarms had been installed. She should have insisted that all nonessential personnel be barred from the estate for the duration. And then, *Thank God, Pierce is safely out of the way,* she thought. She couldn't have kept him safe if he was there with her. He'd have insisted on being macho and male, bum leg and all.

She reached the door without, apparently, alerting anyone inside. Flattening her back against the outside wall of the cabana, just to the side of the door frame, she drew the Baretta out of the holster. Taking a deep breath, she grasped it in both hands in front of her and whirled in front of the door.

Nothing moved.

She waited a minute and then stepped inside.

Still nothing.

She made a slow half circle, the gun held out in front of her. "Lisbeth?" she called, her gaze checking every corner. The cabana was one big room, with a gym on one side and a casual conversation area on the other.

The bathroom and shower area were behind the only other door in the room. It was closed. "Lisbeth?"

Silence.

Nikki lowered her gun and approached the bathroom door. Standing to one side of it, she rapped sharply. "Lisbeth? Are you in there?"

If she was, Nikki thought, she wasn't answering. If she wasn't, then where the hell was she? Nikki reached out and turned the door handle. It opened easily. She pushed it with the muzzle of her gun and, very carefully, peeked around the edge of the door frame.

Lisbeth was lying on the tile floor on her side, apparently unconscious.

"Lisbeth!" Nikki knelt down, the fingers of her free hand automatically searching through the tumbled hair on the girl's neck to feel for a pulse. She found it, finally, beating very faintly, under Lisbeth's fragile jaw.

Nikki shoved her gun into her holster and used both hands to turn the girl over. Her arm flopped across her body as Nikki rolled her onto her back, leaving a trail of blood across the front of her pale yellow blouse. "Good God, what have you done to yourself, Lisbeth?" Nikki breathed, horrified at the sight that greeted her eyes.

The girl had cut both her wrists. And some time ago, too, Nikki thought, because the blood oozing from the lesser cut on her right wrist had already started to coagulate. She hadn't cut it deep enough to sever the vein. The one on her left wrist was more serious. It was still bleeding heavily. Nikki reached up and yanked the towels off the rack next to the shower, using them to wrap Lisbeth's wrists. She fashioned a makeshift bandage for the left one first, making a pad to press against the cut before winding a smaller one around it to hold it in place.

"Hold on, Lisbeth," she said to the unconscious girl as she wrapped a towel around the other wrist. "Just hold on." She jumped up from the floor and ran for the panic button. She hit it with the flat of her hand, made sure it started flashing red, and ran to the door of the cabana. "Kathy," she screamed. "Kathy!"

The secretary stepped out of her office.

"Lisbeth's tried to commit suicide," Nikki said. "I've hit the panic button. Open the front gates so they can get in without any delay," she ordered, disappearing inside the cabana.

She ran back to the bathroom to kneel beside Lisbeth, lifting the girl's head to place a folded towel under it, applying pressure to the seeping wound in her left wrist. "Just hold on a little longer, Lisbeth," she whispered, her fingers against the faint pulse in the girl's neck. "Help is on the way."

She'd wanted to find Pierce's fan and put a stop to her threats but not this way. Not at the cost of a young girl's life. She should have paid more attention to Lisbeth's file; she should have had someone follow up on it, ferret out the circumstances of her previous attempt to take her own life; she should have overridden Pierce's objections and confronted Lisbeth directly. Maybe, then, this wouldn't have happened.

"The gates are open," Kathy said from behind her. "Is she going to be all right?"

"I don't know," Nikki said without looking up. "I hope so."

And then she felt a blinding flash of pain on the back of her head and everything went black.

PIERCE RAMMED the Jaguar through the gates before they were completely open, scraping deep gashes down either side of his sister's car. He didn't even notice. He slammed to a stop behind the limousine in the driveway and jumped out of the car, leaving the door open and the engine running as he staggered up the wide stone steps to the front door.

It was locked.

"Damn it!" he roared, and pounded on the doorbell. "Damn these blasted locks to hell."

Too impatient to wait for someone to let him in, too terrified to wait, he headed around to the back of the house at a painful lope.

He knew who Kathy Frye was now. More importantly, he knew who she used to be. Kay Fielding. He should have recognized the name when Nikki read it to him out of the file, but he hadn't. He'd been so appalled at learning about his secretary's other career as Cherie Bombe that he hadn't paid enough attention to her more recent past.

He'd worked with Kay Fielding.

It had been over fifteen years ago and he'd forgotten about it until that moment in the Jaguar in front of the jewelry store when he'd smelled that perfume again. And finally remembered.

Kay Fielding had had a very small part in *Beyond the Pale*, a movie he'd done when he was barely twenty-one. Her scene had taken one, maybe two days to shoot, if that, and had ended up as thirty seconds on the screen. He'd played a callow, homesick young sailor on leave and she had played the part of the first prostitute he ever visited. It hadn't even been a love scene, just a tawdry depiction of the morning after when, out of guilt, embarrassment and a desperate need to get away from a desperate woman, the young sailor had professed his love.

And she had worn that perfume.

The same perfume she still wore today.

The same perfume that had scented the letters and the charred Barbie doll.

Why in *hell* hadn't he noticed it before, he raged inwardly as he rounded the hedge that shielded the tennis courts from the house. He made a too-sharp turn and slipped on the grass, going down as his bum leg gave out beneath him. He was scrambling to his feet, sweating and swearing, when he saw it. Smoke and flames rising from the cabana.

She'd started another fire.

"*Nikki!*" he roared, and went racing the rest of the way across the yard, tottering crazily, almost falling again with every step as his weight came down on his injured leg. The walking cast hadn't been meant for this kind of treatment.

Kathy came running to meet him. To stop him. "It's too late," she said frantically, grabbing his arm as he was about to enter the burning building. "It's too late. They're gone."

Pierce shook her off. "Let go of me, damn it!" he said, pushing her so hard that she fell to the ground.

Kathy wrapped her arms around his legs. "No, you can't. It's too late."

Ignoring the pain of his injured leg, hardly even feeling it, Pierce reached down, grabbed her by her upper arms with enough force to cause bruises, and peeled her away from him. "If it's really too late, I'll kill you with my bare hands," he swore, and threw her aside like a sack of potatoes.

He didn't pause to see where or how she landed but rushed inside the burning cabana. The smoke wasn't as thick and black this time—there was no smoldering carpet to create that kind of smoke—but there were flames, ravenous flames, licking up the walls.

"Nikki. Damn it, Nikki, where are you? Nikki, *answer me!*"

He heard his name called weakly.

"Where? Nikki, where are you? Call again."

"Here," she choked out. "Here. In front of the bathroom."

He found her on her knees, trying to drag the dead weight of the unconscious Lisbeth across the floor.

"Oh, God!" he swore, and it was a prayer as much as a curse. Was Lisbeth somehow part of this nightmare, after all? "Is she alive?"

"Yes," Nikki gasped between labored breaths. "Barely. Her wrists have been slashed. I don't know if—"

"Tell me later," Pierce ordered, not really listening to what she said. He put his hands on her waist and yanked her upright. "Get out of here." He tossed her bodily toward the door. "I'll take care of Lisbeth." He bent and grabbed her forearms. They slipped out of his hands. He could feel, more than see, the blood that coated them. Nikki's words suddenly made horrible sense, but he didn't have time to be horrified now. He bent lower and hooked his hands under Lisbeth's shoulders. "Damn it," he said, when he realized Nikki had taken a hold of the girl's feet. "I told you to get out of here. Now! I'll take care of Lisbeth."

"No. I won't leave you," Nikki said stubbornly, glaring at him through smoke-induced tears. "You can't do it alone. And I won't leave you."

Knowing it was useless to argue with her, knowing, too, that she might be right, he nodded his head and hefted Lisbeth's limp upper body as Nikki lifted her legs. Together, they started toward the door of the cabana, moving like crabs, scuffling toward light and air and safety.

And Kathy was waiting for them when they got there, madness and rage in her eyes. She launched herself at Nikki like a demented virago. "You can't have him," she screeched, flailing wildly. "I won't let you have him!"

Nikki dropped Lisbeth's feet and fell back under the attack, still dizzy from the blow to the back of her head, disoriented by the smoke pouring out of the cabana, unable to do more than cover her face with her arms.

"You can't have him," Kathy ranted, clawing at Nikki's hair and clothes. "He's mine. He's mine. He loves *me*."

Pierce quickly lowered Lisbeth to the ground and stepped over her, reaching out to grab his secretary by the arms, trying to pull her back, away from Nikki. They scrambled madly for a moment or two, the three of them doing a macabre dance in front of the burning building with the unconscious Lisbeth lying at their feet, until finally, Nikki managed to connect with a well-placed karate chop to Kathy's forearm, breaking her stranglehold. Kathy whirled away, almost too easily. Nikki made an aborted grab for her.

"Look out!" she warned Pierce. "She's got my gun!"

"He's mine," Kathy screamed, both hands wrapped around the butt of the gun as she pointed it at Nikki. Her finger was on the trigger. "He loves me, not you. He loves *me*!"

"Kathy," Pierce said softly, trying to divert her attention to him. He stood tensed and ready, looking for the first opportunity to wrest the gun from her.

She glanced toward him but kept the gun pointed at Nikki.

"Kathy," he crooned softly, "look at me."

The gun wavered in her hands as she turned her head toward him.

"It was just a movie, remember?" he said softly. "We did that scene in *Beyond the Pale* together. Remember? It was just a movie."

"No. You love me," she said. "Me. Tell her."

"What do you want me to tell her?" He edged away from Lisbeth and Nikki as he spoke, his gaze holding Kathy's, trying to keep her attention focused exclusively on him now that he had it. Slowly, very slowly, he held out his hand. "Give me the gun and I'll tell her anything you want me to."

"Tell her you love *me*," she said. "You said you did. Remember? I heard you say it." There was a note of pleading in her voice now, and the gun began to droop in her hand. "Tell her."

Pierce took another half step forward. "Give me the gun first."

His fingers had just touched the muzzle when Lisbeth groaned. Kathy started and jerked the gun upward. Pierce lunged forward in the same instant, his fingers curling around the muzzle. Nikki rushed forward, intent on throwing herself between Pierce and the bullet. The gun went off.

For a moment, nobody moved.

Nobody breathed.

"Pierce?" Nikki whispered fearfully.

"It's all right. The shot went into the ground."

And then Kathy began to sob, a heartbreaking sound of utter hopelessness.

"You said you loved me," she whimpered, crumpling to her knees as she released her hold on the Baretta. "You said it."

Pierce took the gun and handed it to Nikki, then knelt down and took the broken, sobbing woman into his arms, trying vainly to comfort her, knowing there would be no comfort at all for her for a long time to come. "It's going to be all right, Kathy," he said, stroking her hair as she lay, sobbing, against his chest.

Standing there with the gun in her hand and the sound of the approaching sirens screaming in her ears, Nikki watched the man she loved try to comfort the woman who would have killed all three of them if she'd been able, and felt her heart swell with love and pride. She'd fallen for more than just a pretty face this time.

Was that going to make it harder or easier when he walked away?

13

"LISBETH'S GOING to be just fine," Claire said. "The
doctor said the cuts weren't nearly as bad as they
looked. It was the blow to the head that knocked her
out, not the loss of blood. He's going to keep her over-
night for observation. Her aunt's with her now."

"Has somebody called her parents?" Pierce asked,
looking up at his sister.

Claire nodded. "They'll be here tonight."

"I want their airline tickets paid for," Pierce said.
"Hotel, meals, whatever."

Claire nodded.

"And all of Lisbeth's hospital bills."

"Already taken care of," Claire said.

"Mr. Kingston, please," the doctor admonished,
looking up from the plaster cast he was applying to
Pierce's leg. The leg wasn't any more broken than it had
been that morning, but the hope was that a real plaster
cast would make him more careful of it. "You have to
hold still."

"Want me to sit on him?" Gage offered.

Pierce ignored them both. "How's Kathy?"

"She's been sedated," Claire said. "They've got her
in the psychiatric ward, under twenty-four-hour
guard."

Pierce frowned. "Is that necessary?"

"It's mostly to keep out the press," Claire said, "but
it's also partly for her own protection. The psychiatrist

on duty thinks there's a possibly she might try to commit suicide if she isn't watched. In her more lucid moments she seemed to be aware of what she tried to do."

"Which was what, exactly?" Gage asked.

"Well, apparently, she knew all about Lisbeth's background—the failed love affair and the suicide attempt. Although I'm not sure whether it was Lisbeth or Mrs. Gilmore who actually told her. Anyway, when she realized that Nikki suspected Lisbeth of writing the letters, she tried to reenforce that idea by coming up with a false note written on the same paper."

"The note she said she found by the garbage can in the kitchen, that day at lunch," Nikki said.

"Yes. And she was the one who put the blue notepad on the umbrella table with Lisbeth's schoolbooks. She also called Bender Security and rescheduled your appointment with them for later in the day so she could carry out her plan uninterrupted."

"Which was what, exactly?" Pierce asked

"We may never know exactly," Claire said, "but from what I can piece together from what the psychiatrist said, she intended to make it look as if Lisbeth finally went off the deep end and killed Nikki and then, overcome with guilt, slit her own wrists rather than face the consequences."

"What I don't understand," Pierce said, "is why she waited all this time to start writing those letters, why she didn't do it years ago when we did *Beyond the Pale*. That would make more sense, wouldn't it?"

"I asked the psychiatrist that question myself," Claire told him. "He said she's probably had a kind of crush on you since you did the movie together but it only turned obsessive after she started working for you. Apparently seeing you every day, having you smile at her, be nice to her, tease her the way you do everybody…" Claire shook her head sadly. "Given her state of mind, the psychiatrist thinks she would have misinterpreted any halfway friendly gesture on your part to mean you were in love with her."

"What's going to happen to her?" Tara asked.

"There'll be a competency hearing to determine if she's capable of understanding the charges against her."

"I'm not filing charges," Pierce said.

"No, but the state might. Or Lisbeth's parents."

"Then get her a lawyer," Pierce ordered. "She belongs in a mental institution, not a prison."

"Already done," Claire said. "I've also booked her a room in the best private psychiatric hospital in Los Angeles," she added, anticipating her brother's next order. "So she'll be well taken care of." She smiled at him. "Any other questions?"

"Just one." Pierce glared at the doctor from his half-reclining position against the upraised head of the hospital bed. "Are you finished?"

"All finished. As soon as that plaster dries a lit—"

"Everybody out, then," Pierce ordered. "All of you. Out."

Claire raised an elegant eyebrow. "Really, Pierce, don't you think you're being a little—"

"*Out!*" he roared. "No, not you," he said to Nikki, grabbing her hand to keep her where she was. "You stay right here." He looked up at the others standing around the hospital bed: the doctor and nurse, Claire, Tara and Gage. "The rest of you get out."

Gage gave him a knowing grin. "Shall I close the door?" he asked politely, ushering the others out ahead of him.

Pierce gave him a regal nod. "Please."

"Well," Nikki said tartly, "that was extremely rude."

"But effective."

"You want to tell me why?"

"In a minute." He tugged on her hand. "Kiss me first."

"Pierce, this is a hos—"

He reached up, clamping his other hand around the back of her neck, and pulled her head down to his. His lips were hard and possessive, allowing absolutely no resistance. Nikki offered none. Her mouth opened on his, eagerly accepting the thrust of his tongue, avidly offering her own in return. She felt his arms close around her back in a crushing embrace and realized her own were as tightly clasped around his neck. Suddenly, she couldn't get close enough, couldn't taste enough, couldn't feel enough. She arched against him, pressing her breasts against his chest, her body pleading for what her mind hadn't even known she wanted until this very minute.

"Pierce," she moaned against his mouth, her body on fire with the need to be possessed, to physically affirm that they were alive and well and safe. "Oh, Pierce."

"I know, baby. I know. I feel the same way." He caught her hand in his and brought it down between his legs, pressing it against him, leaving no doubt as to his desire for her. "I want that inside you."

She curled her fingers around him. "I want it inside me, too," she whispered achingly, "but . . ."

"Gage locked it."

"What?" she murmured, distracted by the heat and hardness of him.

"The door." The words were whispered into her ear as he fumbled frantically with the buttons of her blouse.

He'd never felt so clumsy in his life, never felt the need for haste so strongly before. "Gage locked it on his way out."

"Are you—" she sighed raggedly as his fingers brushed the bare skin of her belly "—sure?"

"Yes." He unhooked the front clasp of her bra and pushed it aside. "Positive," he said, and bent his head to take her nipple into his mouth.

Nikki cried out, pressing her own mouth against the top of his head to muffle the uncontrollable sounds of passion.

"...get you out of these," he murmured, reaching for the snap on her jeans.

"Yes...yes..." She breathed raggedly, lifting her hips in an effort to accommodate him as he slipped one hand down the back of her jeans to push them off. "Wait, my boots...first...I have to get my—" Her cry of passion was louder this time, jagged and sharp, as he touched the moistness between her legs. Her hands clenched on his shoulders. She began, abruptly, to pant.

"Easy," he murmured, stroking her with the tip of his finger. She was hot and slick, as soft as he was hard. "Easy."

She leaned against him for a moment, panting into his neck, her body buzzing and throbbing and tingling, on the very edge of climax. And then he thrust a finger inside her, just a tiny bit, and she exploded into a thousand pieces.

She pushed her face into his shoulder, hard, feeling the warmth of his neck against her lips, the silkiness of his hair against her cheek, and an aching, throbbing emptiness deep inside her. She pulled away from him abruptly, unable to bear it another minute. She yanked off her boots and then her jeans and panties, peeling them down her legs with frantic haste, leaving them in a pile on the floor as she climbed back onto the bed and swung one long leg over his hips.

He'd already yanked his hospital gown up and pushed his black silk briefs down, just enough to free his straining erection. He put his hands on her hips, guiding her as she sank down on him. They both groaned as if mortally wounded, neither of them caring, or even aware, of what sounds might carry beyond the locked door of the room. She lifted herself on her knees, once . . . twice . . . a third time, and then his hands spasmed on her hips hard enough to leave bruises and her head fell back and they rocketed through the universe together. The entire world could have come into the room at that moment and neither of them would have noticed, or cared, so great was their concentration on each other and the emotion ricocheting between them.

They held each other tight as they came drifting back to earth—his arms locked around the small of her back, his head nestled against her breasts; her arms around his neck, her cheek pressed to his hair. They clung together until their hearts slowed to nearly normal and their breathing became more regular and the fierce panic of near loss receded to manageable levels.

Nikki was the first to stir. She sat up, putting her hands on his shoulders to push herself away from him. "I'd better get dressed," she murmured, embarrassed now by her uninhibited display of passion.

"Not yet," Pierce said, letting her move only so far, and then no further.

"Pierce," she protested softly.

"Not yet, sweetheart." He curled his finger under her chin. "Look at me, Nikki. Come on, don't be shy. Look at me. I have something I want to say to you."

She peeked up at him from under her lashes. "What?"

"Something to ask you, really," he said, hedging.

She lifted her head a little higher. "What?"

"It's not exactly how I'd planned to say it but . . ."

She looked straight at him. "What?"

He was the one who looked away now. "I wanted there to be champagne and music and flowers. You know, all the trimmings but—"

"Pierce—" she put her hands on either side of his face and made him look at her "—*what*?"

They stared at each other for a long intense moment, laser blue eyes gazing into pale, pure green. Eyes full of questions and doubts and fears. And love. Oceans of love. Endless love.

Keeping one arm around her, Pierce reached sideways for the raw silk jacket draped over the chair next to the bed. One-handed, he fumbled for the inside pocket, finally pulling out a tiny velvet box. He flipped it open with his thumb.

"Will you marry me?" he asked.

Nikki blinked, looking back and forth between him and the ring. "Oh, Pierce," she said, awed by both. She'd been expecting a suggestion that they continue their affair. Or an invitation to move in with him until it had run its course. But this . . . She was overwhelmed. "Oh, Pierce."

"Is that a yes?"

"I . . ." Her eyes were misty as she stared at him. "I don't know what to say."

"Say yes," he ordered.

"But I . . . you . . ."

"I . . . you . . . what?" he asked.

"You can't mean it."

"What do you mean, I can't mean it?" He was beginning to get irritated. "Of course, I mean it."

"But you're *you*. You're Pierce Kingston, the rich, famous movie star. And I'm . . . I'm just—"

"You're beautiful and smart and brave," he said, suddenly understanding. His arms closed tight around her. "And you're the woman I love more than anyone or anything in the world. You're the only woman I've ever loved." He stared into her eyes as he said it. "The only woman I *will* ever love."

"Oh, Pierce."

His lips curved into a loving smile. "Is that a yes?"

"Yes," she said, before he could ask again. "Yes. Yes. *Yes!*"

He hugged her hard and then let go of her to take the ring out of the box. "Here," he said, sliding it onto the ring finger of her left hand before she could change her mind. "Put it on."

"Oh, Pierce."

They both stared down at it, entranced, and then looked up again to smile mistily at each other.

"You know what this means, don't you?" Nikki asked, looking back down at the ring.

"No, what?" he asked, although he knew perfectly well.

"It means I've gone and fallen for another pretty face."

Pierce grinned his pirate's grin. "Just so long as it's the last pretty face you fall for," he said sternly, and wrapped his arms around her to begin the loving all over again.

Coming Attractions

Don't miss the third and final book in the blockbuster Hollywood Dynasty mini-series, *The Right Direction*! You've already got the scoop on Gage and Pierce Kingston's troubles and triumphs as members of a legendary movie-making family in *The Other Woman* and *Just Another Pretty Face*. In October, you'll get a chance to learn the inside story on their sister, Claire Kingston.

In *The Right Direction*, cool, controlled producer Claire Kingston decides to gamble by hiring Hollywood's hot bad boy, director Rafe Santana, for her next film. It's instant combustion when the filming of the movie that could make or break both their careers begins.

FOR BETTER
FOR WORSE

They would each face life's bittersweet choices in their search for love...

Penny Jordan has created a masterpiece of raw emotion, with this dramatic novel which takes a fascinating and, at times, painfully telling look at three couples' hopes, dreams and desires.

A story of obsessions...
A story of choices...
A story of love.

AVAILABLE NOW

PRICED: £4.99

W★RLDWIDE

Spoil yourself next month
with these four novels from

Temptation

THE RIGHT DIRECTION by Candace Schuler

The final part of this blockbusting **Hollywood Dynasty** trilogy.

Rumour had it that renegade film director, Rafe Santana, was
melting Ice Queen, Claire Kingston's, heart. Their combustible
combination promised to generate more heat and hype than the
movie they were working on itself. But would their affair last
beyond the final take?

THE PIRATE'S WOMAN by Madeline Harper

He was standing over her when Diana Tremont regained
consciousness. But her handsome, sexy, charming date was
now acting like a barbarian! Adam Hawke claimed he was
Captain Hawke, and she was his defenceless captive…

THE SPY WHO LOVED HER by Sheryl Danson

Tough, cynical special agent Alex Sullivan thought a little
assignment rescuing blonde, blue-eyed Megan Davies from a
war zone ought to have been a snap. But he hadn't anticipated
Megan's stubbornness, nor her warm, enticing sexiness.

MESSAGE FOR JESSE by Patricia Coughlin

The minute Jesse McPherson came into view, Kali Spencer
was hooked. But what was the secret to attracting his
attention? This gorgeous, impatient, *impossible* man was
avoiding her. Kali had no choice but to woo him in the most
outrageous ways imaginable…

NORA ROBERTS

◆

SWEET REVENGE

Adrianne's glittering lifestyle was the perfect foil for her extraordinary talents — no one knew her as *The Shadow*, the most notorious jewel thief of the decade. She had a secret ambition to carry out the ultimate heist — one that would even an old and bitter score. But she would need all her stealth and cunning to pull it off, with Philip Chamberlain, Interpol's toughest and smartest cop, hot on her trail. His only mistake was to fall under Adrianne's seductive spell.

AVAILABLE NOW   **PRICE £4.99**

WORLDWIDE